Dandelions

DANDELIONS

Yasunari Kawabata

*Translated and with an afterword
by Michael Emmerich*

A NEW DIRECTIONS PAPERBOOK ORIGINAL

Published by arrangement with Chuokoron-Shinsha and the Wylie Agency. This translation is based on the text of *Tampopo* in *Kawabata Yasunari zenshū* (Shinchōsa, 1980).

First published as a New Directions Paperbook (NDP1393) in 2017
Manufactured in the United States of America
New Directions Books are printed on acid-free paper
Design by Erik Rieselbach

Library of Congress Cataloging-in-Publication Data
Names: Kawabata, Yasunari, 1899–1972, author. |
Emmerich, Michael, translator.
Title: Dandelions / Yasunari Kawabata ; translated by Michael Emmerich.
Other titles: Tampopo. English
Description: New York : New Directions Publishing Corporation, 2017.
Identifiers: LCCN 2017014026 | ISBN 9780811224093 (alk. paper)
Subjects: LCSH: Distress (Psychology)—Fiction. | Desire—Fiction. |
Psychological fiction.
Classification: LCC PL832.A9 T313 2017 | DDC 895.63/44—dc23
LC record available at https://lccn.loc.gov/2017014026

10 9 8 7 6 5 4 3 2

New Directions Books are published for James Laughlin
by New Directions Publishing Corporation
80 Eighth Avenue, New York 10011

Dandelions

DANDELIONS COVER THE banks of Ikuta River. They are an expression of the town's character—Ikuta is like springtime, when the dandelions bloom. Three hundred and ninety four of its thirty-five thousand residents are over eighty years old.

Only one thing seems out of place in this town: the madhouse. Though maybe it helps for a madhouse to be in such incongruous surroundings. Perhaps whoever chose to put one here, in this quiet, sleepy, graying town, was a sage. Not that every disturbed mind can be cured by peaceful surroundings: the mad inhabit their own worlds, detached from reality, and a simple change of scenery doesn't usually have much of an effect on that. Staying at the clinic, here in Ikuta, probably does less for the patients themselves than the town does for the people who bring them. Madness is more idiosyncratic than sanity; no single cure suits all patients.

The families and friends of the mad are blessed, however, by the bright landscape and the welcoming, dandelion-like glow of the town, which blunts their guilt—no, they were not abandoning their loved ones, locking them away in the sort of cruel, desolate environment that comes to mind when one thinks of an insane asylum. As they walk down the path on the riverbank after leaving their lunatic in the clinic on the hill, they hear behind them the long, low gonging of the temple bell. It's as if the one they had left behind is calling to them, saying goodbye. As if the bell is being struck to mark their parting. Forlorn but not unsettled, its ringing passes over the town and heads out to sea. Nothing in the sound suggests that the person striking it is deranged.

The doctor mentioned the bell as Kizaki Ineko's mother and Ineko's lover, Kuno, were on their way out, leaving Ineko behind.

"If you hear the bell as you go," he said, "assume it's her ringing it."

"Excuse me?" Ineko's mother said, nonplussed.

"We'll have your daughter ring the three o'clock bell today."

"Ah."

"One day we let the patients strike the bell, and they all got so excited ... Now more of them want to ring it each day than we can possibly manage. Some patients ask us to let them strike it when they've recovered, as a way of marking the end of their stay. And we like to let new patients strike the bell when they join us, unless their symptoms are too severe. Naturally, the nurses stay with them, and not many of our patients are in such dire straits that striking a bell would be too much for them. Your daughter's symptoms for instance are quite mild."

"Yes."

"We think there may be something therapeutic in ringing the bell. Of course, we can't be sure—this isn't surgery or internal medicine, after all. Sometimes you think they've gotten better, only to have things take a sudden turn for the worse, and in many cases you can't even identify the cause of their illness. Some of our younger doctors, though, insist they can tell just from the sound of the bell how a patient is doing."

"Oh?"

"The ringing is definitely telling us something, that's for sure. You hear something coming from deep within them, perhaps—deep in their hearts."

"Is that so?" Kuno nodded, eyeing the doctor a bit skeptically.

"As you know, our patients are isolated from the world. But when they strike the bell, the sound carries beyond the clinic, all through town. Whether or not they realize it, our patients are addressing themselves to the outside world. Or, to put it in slightly grandiose terms, by ringing that bell, they're reminding the world that they're here—that they exist."

"It sounds kind of sad when you put it like that," said Ineko's mother.

"Sad? I wouldn't say that," said the doctor. "After all, the people of Ikuta have no way of knowing who is striking the bell—I doubt they even wonder. All they hear is the hour. It's such a part of everyday life now, I'm sure they've forgotten that the people ringing it are crazy. They don't notice how the tone shifts, or how it reveals the things our patients hold in their hearts—it's a timepiece, nothing more. And yet it's part of their landscape, the ringing of the Ikuta Clinic bell."

"............"

"The priests used to strike the bell once at six in the morning and then again at six in the evening. Striking it was such a delight for our patients, though, that we asked the town to let us ring it five times a day—at six and eleven in the morning, three and six in the afternoon, and then once more at nine in the evening. Not many towns have bells five times a day. Some of the townspeople were against the nine o'clock bell, but it helps our patients prepare for bedtime, and it's such a tranquil, peaceful sound that the town agreed."

Ineko's mother and lover gazed down at Ikuta from the clinic's doorway.

"It's such a nice, easygoing town," Ineko's mother said. "I doubt anyone living in a place like this would ever succumb to a peculiar condition like body blindness."

"Your daughter's condition is extraordinarily rare, it's true," said the doctor. "None of us has ever encountered a case of somagnosia before."

Ikuta Clinic stood on the grounds of Jōkōji, a dilapidated temple with hardly any income, as the priests' decision to allow an insane asylum within its precincts made clear. Nowadays it almost seemed as though the temple was on the grounds of the clinic. Patients didn't just strike the bell; as long as there was no danger of their turning violent or running away, they could roam freely in the garden and go up into the temple's main hall, where they did handicrafts and other such things, just as they pleased.

Old Nishiyama, for instance, who had lived so long in the clinic he seemed like its master, often spread sheets of paper on the tatami floor to practice his calligraphy, writing very large characters. The mad old man hardly ever had plain white paper, whether Japanese or Chinese, so most of the time he used old newspaper.

He almost always wrote the same eight-character phrase: *To enter the Buddha world is easy; to enter the world of demons is difficult.* His sight was clouded by cataracts, but the calligraphy was forceful. There was nothing mundane about it, and nothing showy either. Only, perhaps, a hint of madness. The characters were neither loud nor disturbed in any clichéd way, but if you looked carefully you began to sense something maniacal in them, something demonic. Maybe there had been a time in Old Nishiyama's life when he tried to enter the world of demons, but he found it too difficult, and the agony of that failure gave the calligraphy of his lunatic old age its flavor. Whatever form his "world of demons" may have taken, his determination to enter it caused him such pain that it cost him his sanity. From his point of view, the asylum bore no resemblance to the world of demons, but it probably also never occurred to him to consider it a refuge, a place of rest for those who tried and failed to enter that other world.

Nowadays, Old Nishiyama was among the clinic's quietest patients. He had lost his teeth and had never gotten dentures, so his cheeks were sunken; he was bald apart from a fuzz of soft white hair at the back of his head. It was hard to imagine, looking at him, that he would have the strength for anything demonic—it was only in his writing, you might say, that traces of that spirit lingered. The old man tended to lose his temper during calligraphy practice, but in so mild a manner that it probably wouldn't have been a problem even in an ordinary old people's home.

Old Nishiyama looked forward to the weather report on the radio every day, before the seven o'clock news. He had no interest in the information itself—warnings for instance that it would be a bit windy and choppy on the ocean tonight and tomorrow, with poor visibility from the fog. What he loved was the voice of the young woman who read it out. She sounded marvelously gentle, her tone soft but not too soft. The old man felt as if this charming young woman were speaking directly to him from the world outside the asylum. Her voice brimmed with love. It was a comfort to the old man, a consolation. It was an echo of the gorgeous days of his youth. He didn't know her name, he'd never seen her, and no doubt she would go on broadcasting the weather in that lovely voice long after he was dead, but none of that mattered to Old Nishiyama: she was the only one who talked to him, to the wreck he had become, day after day, with love in her voice.

The patients showed Old Nishiyama a certain deference; few crazies ever tried to strike up a conversation. Kizaki Ineko had a lovely voice, so he might be pleased if she were to strike up a friendship. Perhaps that would have led in an odd direction, though. Afflicted as she was with somagnosia, she might not have seen Old Nishiyama's body at all—just a brush gliding across the paper, tracing those eight characters: *To enter the Buddha world is easy; to enter the world of demons is difficult.* And if Old Nishiyama were somehow to discover his own invisibility to Ineko—that all she saw were his brush and the characters it traced—maybe he'd leap for joy, believing that at last he had gained entry to the demonic world. Or maybe he wouldn't … perhaps it was a mistake to assume that his "world of demons" could ever assume so mild a form. Of course, it was possible, too, that as his spirit succumbed to the ravages of old age, so too did his "world of demons." Perhaps a few moments with the youthful Ineko would be all it would take to transport him there. Maybe reaching his "world of demons" was no longer so difficult that just trying would cost him his sanity.

Jōkōji stands at the top of a hill to the north of Ikuta. The hill is small, but Ikuta River still has to curve around its base to go on. Ikuta River, too, is small. The water only comes up about shin-high; even at the delta you can wade from one side to the other. It is about ten paces across. On one bank there is a path, too narrow for cars.

Having descended the hill from Jōkōji and the Ikuta Clinic, Ineko's mother and Ineko's lover Kuno set out along the path in the direction that led to the ocean. They were heading for the train station.

"What do you think that big tree by her door to the room was, Mr. Kuno?" Ineko's mother asked. "What type of oak, I mean?"

"I didn't notice it, I'm afraid."

"It's hard to tell without the leaves."

"Ah."

"It was big for a natural tree. So you didn't notice, Mr. Kuno, that it was crying?"

"The tree was crying?"

"To me they looked like tears. It had scars all down its trunk. I'm sure the lunatics must have carved them, though I can't imagine with what since surely they aren't allowed to keep knives. The cracked bark has grown so thick, like the shell of an old turtle covered with moss, that it would take considerable strength and persistence to make cuts so deep. It looked as if some of the lunatics had carved their names, though I didn't get a good enough look to say for sure. Why do you suppose people who have lost their minds would want to carve their names, Mr. Kuno, on a tree in the asylum that houses them?"

"Hard to say. Maybe because they're in an asylum. And because the tree's there." Kuno paused and thought. "Does that count as an answer? Sometimes people just want to leave a mark, to prove to themselves that they were there at that moment, wherever they are—an asylum or someplace else."

"Ineko will never be able to erase the fact that she spent part of her life there, at Ikuta Clinic. Even if she doesn't carve her name on the tree."

"Mother, you thought that the tree was weeping for the lunatics?"

"No." Ineko's mother shook her head. "It was crying from the cuts they made in its bark. When you slice deep enough, a thick liquid oozes out of the trunk—sap, I guess it's called. The sap trickled into the cuts and hardened there, like lines of wax down a candle. I thought it looked like the tree had been weeping—not for the lunatics, but because of them."

It was February. From the end of last year, dandelions had begun blooming in the sunny spots in Ikuta—a town that was itself like a spot of sunlight. There wasn't any sign of spring yet in the color of the grass on the riverbanks. But bright blue flowers, small, ever so small—what were they called?—bloomed there unobtrusively, like a harbinger of spring.

Kuno was gazing at the river. Suddenly he cried out:

"A white rat! Look, Mother—on the other shore, over there."

"A white rat?" Ineko's mother looked where Kuno pointed but saw nothing moving.

"You don't see it?"

"No."

They had stopped walking.

"You said it was a white rat, Mr. Kuno?" Ineko's mother said. "Doesn't that seem odd? There's no such thing as a white rat."

"It certainly looked like a white rat. It darted off through the grass."

"A white rat couldn't possibly be living out here, in the wild. I wonder what it could have been ... a white animal, not a rat but about that size, around here?"

"I wonder."

"There are no such animals here."

"When you put it like that, I suppose not." Kuno blinked his eyes, then scanned the far shore. "Maybe it's me. What could it have been? Maybe it's me, going crazy."

"No, it isn't that," Ineko's mother said. "After such a short visit to the asylum."

"A visit to the asylum?" Kuno said sharply. "We took Ineko, that's all, as you know; we just left her there." He looked at her face—the mother. "I'm sorry, Mother. You're her mother, of course."

". . . . ."

"Ah." Kuno lifted his left hand. "I see now. The tree was weeping … the tree that cried because the lunatics made it, that was Ineko?"

"The tree was Ineko? That never even crossed my mind. I just noticed the tree, that's all—and then I saw the cuts in its trunk."

"I didn't notice the big tree at the clinic; I saw a white rat on the far bank. You didn't see the rat, so it doesn't exist. Just as the tree, whatever kind of oak it was, isn't there for me."

"That's absurd. A tree doesn't move like a rat—showing itself one instant and hiding the next. That tree will always be there beside her door. Until someone cuts it down, or it withers and dies. Unless the lunatics come in a mob and hack right through that thick trunk."

"A lunatic revolt?"

"They wouldn't do that, would they."

"Of course, the mad are stronger, individually, than the sane. Though I bet if anyone ever got his hands on a saw and started going at that trunk, it'd spread in a flash—everyone rushing to join the fray. There would be blood, I'm sure, with everyone grabbing the saw."

"Terrible, when the tree is crying already." Ineko's mother blinked sadly. "Besides, if they chopped the tree down, they couldn't scar its trunk anymore to prove they're alive."

"It isn't necessary."

"Let's not talk about it. That tree must have been there for decades, for more than a century, before the clinic was built, seeing how big it is. I'm quite sure you'll notice it, Mr. Kuno, should you be so kind as to go pay Ineko a visit."

"Of course. I won't even have to notice it; I'll keep an eye out, now that you've told me. I'll probably try to read the names on its trunk, too. And see the tears."

"I'm sure you will. You'll never see another white rat, though, even when you walk up to the clinic and back, along this bank."

"What makes you so sure? You think there aren't any here to begin with?"

"No, it's not that. There aren't, of course. But even if there were."

"I just wouldn't see them?"

"............"

Three girls in school uniforms came riding up on their bicycles from the ocean. There was probably room to share the path, but Kuno and the mother stepped off to the side nearer the river and waited for them to pass. Each girl nodded as she went by. Their cheeks were as flushed as if they had come from a walk along the shore in winter, despite the town's warmth. They were pedaling upriver, seemingly headed up the hill toward the Ikuta Clinic. A grove of bamboo grew at the foot of the hill. A faint column of smoke drifted up from the bamboo. The house where they were burning leaves, or whatever it was they were burning, was hidden. The clinic, too, was concealed among the trees at the top of the hill.

"You know, Mother," Kuno said. "I'm thinking I'd like to go back to the clinic and have a look at that tree. I feel like I won't be able to get it out of my mind if I leave without seeing it. And that makes me uneasy—the idea of being unable to forget something I haven't seen. If I just dash up now, I'll still make the train."

"The tree will be there next time, Mr. Kuno, just as it is now," the mother said. "It's always there, and will be forever. Even after Ineko gets better and checks out."

"If only you and the clinic doctors would give me permission, I'd like to marry Ineko and live with her there at the asylum. I'm sorry, that didn't come out quite right ... I would like to stay there and give her the care she needs."

"No, no, Mr. Kuno, we couldn't have that."

"I let you get the better of me, I didn't hold my ground, and now we've gone and left her in an asylum. Postponing the wedding makes a certain amount of sense, even if you're just being overcautious. But I'm amazed you decided to separate her from me. Committing her to the asylum, leaving her there all alone. An asylum is like the bottom of a pool where all the toxins in the human heart accumulate, bubbling and seething. All those toxins surrounding Ineko, eating into her. Imagine it, Mother—if the lunatics grew agitated, if they did something to harm her, Ineko, our beautiful pearl ..."

"Nonsense." the mother cut him off. "There is order in the clinic, and iron bars."

"You're the one who said the tree was crying because the lunatics cut it up. You're the one who wondered if they might go wild and chop it down." Kuno gazed at Ineko's mother. "The tree is Ineko, isn't it? The tree that looked to you like it was weeping."

"A tree's tears are just sap. Ineko didn't shed a tear."

"She's going to get better quickly and come home, that's what she said. The tears were there, streaming from the back of her eyes into her heart." Once more, Kuno turned to look back from where they had come. "I can see the hill with the clinic, but not Ineko. She really is there, isn't she? Among the trees, and the lunatics? I'd like to go back and check."

"............"

"I begged you not to put her in the asylum, to let me marry her instead."

"Mr. Kuno, you remember what the doctor in Tokyo said. About the young somagnosic mother who killed her child. How she stopped seeing her baby's head, and killed it."

"That was an infant. Cover a newborn's mouth for a few seconds and that's it—it's dead. Just stepping on it will kill it. I'm not an infant," said Kuno. "Ineko's attacks won't kill me. I'm strong enough to restrain her."

"I never thought she'd kill you. But she might have a child."

"............"

"That somagnosic mother put her hands around her baby's invisible neck and strangled it. How is that possible? To be unable to see your own baby's head, to wring a neck that isn't even visible to you. Just hearing the story made me shudder."

"I was right there with you, listening to that doctor, and I thought that the woman's family should have been more careful. Someone should always have been there, watching."

"It was her first episode. They couldn't have known."

The week after she killed her baby, the woman had been transferred from the maternity ward to a mental hospital. Kuno and Ineko's mother had heard her story from a doctor at a psychiatric ward in Tokyo. The doctor hadn't known how to answer when Kuno asked the obvious question about why the woman stopped seeing the baby's head when she could see everything else—though perhaps this, too, was only to be expected.

"Was it the intensity of her love, was it too extreme?" Kuno asked, "Surely it wasn't an intense, extreme hatred?"

The doctor couldn't really say. Madness, he explained, could stem from other emotions, too, not just love and hate.

"Can you imagine a baby being so adorable, so utterly adorable that you just keep staring and staring until it dissolves away, and you don't see it anymore?" asked Kuno.

"Yes, I can. But that much seems normal."

A normal person, suddenly realizing she couldn't see her baby's head, might, in her shock and horror, seize hold of it, but she would let go before the baby died.

"How many minutes did she keep her hands around the baby's neck?" Kuno asked. "How long was the head invisible?"

"It's impossible to say. No one else was there, after all," the doctor said. "Long enough for the demon to do its work."

"The demon?" Kuno asked, surprised. "Are there demons in medicine?"

"Everywhere you look. Especially for someone like me, in psychiatry—I spend most of my time dealing with the moments when they show themselves. Sometimes I think that's all human existence is. One such moment after the next."

"What rubbish," Kuno muttered. Then, "Listen, I came to see you because I want to cure Ineko's somagnosia through marriage, and I believe I can. I'd be grateful if you could at least assure Ineko's mother that there's no reason Ineko can't marry, and tell her that marriage can sometimes work wonders. Maybe you can get her to come around."

The truth was, of course, that even a doctor's encouragement was unlikely to help Ineko's mother overcome her reluctance to allow the marriage. Ineko had never become blind to any other person she was with; it had happened for the first time with Kuno. Perhaps he himself had somehow triggered the condition. And then the doctor had gone and told the mother what had happened next, after that young woman killed her baby—that she had gone stark raving mad. His story left Ineko's mother in a state of terror.

The same doctor had introduced the Ikuta Clinic, and helped the mother decide to commit her daughter. Truth be told, there'd never been much of a chance that she would be swayed by Kuno's entreaties, by the earnestness of his desire to keep Ineko out free.

Still, she had needed him to go with her to Ikuta. His presence at her side as they walked back from the clinic without Ineko provided, she felt, the spiritual support she required. Her body brimmed with affection for him, as if by walking together she and Kuno could share the burden of her daughter's fate.

Again the mother stopped walking. "You commented earlier that you could see the hill with the clinic, but not Ineko. It's not nice of you to say such odd things, Mr. Kuno. Now I can't stop thinking about it."

"There's nothing odd in that. It's just as I said."

"You can't see the clinic through the trees, and you can't see Ineko inside the clinic either, not from here. That goes without saying."

"That's what's been scaring me lately—the notion that something exists, but you can't see it."

"That's nothing like somagnosia, like someone vanishing right in front of you."

"No, it isn't. But can you tell me what Ineko is doing now, Mother, at this moment? Can you describe her to me, when we can't see her? Please, I've got to go back to the clinic."

"If we went back, Ineko would think she's worse than she realized."

"I could peek in at her, that would be fine. I'd like to see that big tree you said was crying, too," Kuno said restlessly. "When I'm here with you, Mother, even our shadows are clearly visible, yours and mine. I don't want to be separated from Ineko."

Ineko's mother looked down. She realized, seeing how far their shadows stretched in the winter afternoon light, how late it was: they went all the way to the river's edge, breaking at the top of the bank; the shapes seemed unsettled. She made sure, as they walked on, that their shadows didn't overlap.

There was a bridge at the end of the river over which the road to the station passed. The bridge crossed the river's mouth, but from here it seemed to arc over the ocean itself. You could see ocean under the bridge. The river was no wider there than upstream, and where it flowed into the ocean there was nothing to see; the banks were a little lower, that was all. Both the ocean and the sky were peaceful.

They heard the temple bell.

"Ah, the bell," Kuno said. "That's Ineko."

"Ineko's bell." The mother glanced at her watch. "Three o'clock. The doctor said he would let her ring the bell at three."

They turned back toward the hill and raised their eyes. The tolling seemed to come from the sky, and stay in the sky. A temple in a country town like this one was unlikely to have a large and celebrated bell, but it was probably old enough. Its tone was dry rather than hard, with a gravely vibration at the tail. Even after it had faded imperceptibly into silence, the mood it created lingered in their hearts. The town seemed to have no sound. Neither the small river nor the ocean made any noise.

"It's so still now, it's like time has stopped," Kuno said. "As if the flow of time itself is waiting, hushed, in the interval between Ineko's first strike and the next."

The bell rang out a second time.

"She struck it on her own that time. I'm sure of it," Kuno said. "It sounded even weaker than the first one, don't you think?"

The mother nodded silently, trying to hear the bell deep in her ears.

Kuno continued. "The doctor said the nurses help the patients swing the striker. The first time they hold onto the rope with the patient, pulling it back and striking the bell together. And then the second time ... *Here, go ahead and try it yourself.*"

"You sound as if you're seeing it." Ineko's mother smiled.

"Or maybe Ineko asked the nurse to let her strike it alone. You know what just occurred to me, though?" Kuno said, his voice louder than before. "We should have gone over to see the temple's bell tower—if we had, we'd feel like we could see her, even from here."

"Ineko rang a temple bell once. Where was that, I wonder?" The mother's eyes seemed to turn toward the past. "Oh, I know. It was Miidera. We'd gone sightseeing in Kyoto, and we went down to Lake Biwa to go around the Eight Views of Ōmi. You've heard of the evening bell at Miidera? They let visitors strike it for a fee. That really was a massive old bell—every bit as big as you'd expect at a temple like that."

"When was that? How old would Ineko have been?"

"She was in middle school. Yes, it was the year she started."

"You went in the spring? To celebrate her getting in?"

"It was winter. I remember we had duck hot pot at a restaurant they had built out over the lake, in a room with a tatami floor. It was near the end of the year. Sometimes Ineko still talks about the duck we had that time. I guess it made an impression, looking out over the wintry lake from that room. All that water under a low, cloudy sky. It was as cold on the lake as it had been in Kyoto."

"Ineko must have been adorable then, in her first year of middle school."

"She was a child."

"If only you had introduced us then, Mother, when she was still a child. Then she would have felt a different sort of affection for me, she wouldn't have had to hold back, and I bet she would never have come down with somagnosia."

"Don't speak nonsense," the mother said, eyeing Kuno. "Just imagine her then, in middle school." The bell rang a third time then, and she stopped.

"She struck that one by herself, too," Kuno said.

"How many times will she strike it?" Ineko's mother murmured.

"I doubt there's a limit. They've got lunatics hitting it, after all," Kuno said nonchalantly. "They probably let them strike it as many times as they like."

"You can't keep ringing a bell forever."

"I bet Ineko will keep at it for at least as long as you and I are walking on this riverbank, so it's like she's calling goodbye to us, since she knows we can hear."

"That's ridiculous. She'd collapse from exhaustion."

"If she gets worn out, we'll hear it in the bell's tone. Didn't the doctor say striking the bell is a kind of therapy? That you can tell how a patient is doing from the sound."

"He wasn't so definitive. He said *maybe* you could tell."

The gonging came again. The unevenness of the rings, both their spacing and their force, proved that the person swinging the striker was inexperienced, and suggested Kuno had been right to infer that Ineko was striking it alone. Presumably the nurse was just standing nearby, keeping an eye on her.

"Mother," Kuno began, then paused, unable to go on. "Ineko will start crying before she finishes ringing the bell. I'm sure she will. Of course she will."

"Why Mr. Kuno, didn't you just say it's therapeutic? Maybe each time she strikes the bell the ringing draws out a bit of whatever it is that's clouding her mind, the smudges in her head, and then those clouds just disappear into the sky."

"The sound of the bell speaks the emotions of the patient who strikes it. There's only one bell hanging in the temple, and yet the sound alters with each person who strikes it."

"At least when the patient's family is listening, as they are now."

"Let's go back, Mother," Kuno urged, "back to the clinic, while Ineko is still striking the bell. Think how lonely she'll feel when it's exhausted her, when the ringing stops—and how lonely you and I will feel. She's striking the bell to see us off, but that ringing is the sound of her calling us back. If we don't go, Ineko might just go on swinging the striker at the bell until she collapses in a faint. There, it rang again. She's calling us."

"There's a nurse with her, Mr. Kuno. We mustn't lose our heads," said the mother sternly. "I'm grateful, as her mother, that you say such things. But how do you think this would turn out if I were to let you stay with Ineko, even marry her, when you talk like that?"

"I would settle down. At the very least, it would be better for Ineko than the asylum."

The mother walked on four or five steps, her head bent.

"Please don't take this badly. What if, speaking hypothetically..."

"Hypothetically?" Kuno said.

"Never mind."

"No, go on."

"What if, speaking hypothetically, you and she were together, physically, and she stopped seeing your body? Wouldn't you mind? If she couldn't see your face, your hands …"

"That wouldn't bother me."

"But don't you think it would make her even crazier? Oh, how awful it would be! Of course, I can't imagine she'd be strong enough to kill you."

"We've done something similar," Kuno said. "I'd ask her to cover her eyes. Either way, it doesn't really matter. You know what I mean … women close their eyes."

"Now really." The mother's face flushed, as if she were blushing on Ineko's behalf. Then the moment passed. "You said something silly earlier, too, Mr. Kuno. Something nonsensical. That I should have introduced you when she was a girl, when she rang the bell at Miidera."

"Why is that nonsensical?"

"Well, isn't it? Ineko was in middle school, she had never met you, never even heard your name. And you, too—you didn't know she was alive. To put it as you did before, as far as each of you was concerned, the other might as well not have existed."

"That's an odd thought. Seeing as we were both alive and well."

"Until you met, of course. There's really nothing odd about that—no one can meet everyone who was born at the same they were."

"But if we were going to meet anyway, why not bring us together sooner? That's what I don't understand."

"Now you're being silly. That's like saying … well, this is an utterly absurd example, but say you and Ineko were to marry someday, and you had a child—it would be like sitting that child down and saying, *If you were going to be born anyway, why weren't you born five or six years earlier?*"

"That's not the same at all. An unborn baby doesn't yet exist. But Ineko and I were both here, in this world—she was Ineko, and I was me. We just didn't exist for each other. It's strange, but that's how it was."

"If you had known Ineko when she was small, though ... who knows, Mr. Kuno. Maybe you wouldn't have fallen in love with her."

"You have a shallow heart."

"What?" The mother was clearly taken aback. "I think people meet when the time is right, don't you?"

All throughout their conversation, Ineko's bell had gone on ringing.

"Tell me, Mother," Kuno said. "Do you suppose Ineko is thinking of that time at Miidera, when she was a girl? While she's ringing the bell now? I bet she is, poor thing."

"Ah, Miidera ..." the mother replied. "She remembers it, I'm sure. We hardly ever went on trips together, you know, all three of us. Her father was alive then, he took us. We walked out from the bell tower to a spot where you could look out over everything, and there was Lake Biwa and all the buildings along the shore. The sky had a chill look to it."

"Ineko's father died three years later, is that right?" Kuno asked, though he already knew the answer.

"Yes. Ineko must have told you?"

"She did."

"She was there when it happened. He fell off a cliff into the ocean." Kuno nodded.

"To this day, she blanches and starts trembling whenever she sees a horse."

It happened on the west coast of the Izu Peninsula, on a road that hadn't yet seen local bus traffic or sightseeing tours. Ineko and her father were traveling on horseback.

During the war, the father, Kizaki, had been a commissioned officer in the army during the war. His entire right leg was prosthetic, right up to the hip. He had been hurt fighting the Americans in the Philippines, and they amputated. He was serving again in Kagoshima at the time of Japan's unconditional surrender. You would have thought that as an officer with only one leg he would have been allowed to retire for good, but they had called him back—perhaps because the military was understaffed, and perhaps, too, because he had experience planning guerrilla warfare in the mountains of China and the Philippines. If the Americans ever came ashore in Kyūshū, he was to command a guerilla unit made up of both soldiers and civilians. He had to know the land inside and out, so he'd mount his horse and ride all over the island, through the fields and over the peaks. Naturally, he never shied from paths that should have been too steep and treacherous for a man straddling a horse with a fake leg—paths that hardly deserved the name. He was confident in his horsemanship.

When Japan surrendered on August 15, Kizaki abandoned his men, galloping off on his well-loved horse. It was rumored that he had ridden up into the mountains he had studied so well to find some secret spot to end his life, although as a superior officer this was hardly a responsible course of action. Then, five days later, he returned. He and his horse both looked haggard, and he had grown a beard. Ineko was three at the time.

Two years later, Kizaki rather grudgingly went to work as an instructor at a riding club in Tokyo after a friend silently pulled strings on his behalf and urged him to accept the post. The whole country was still sunk in the numbness, poverty, and turmoil that followed the defeat, and so many horses had died during the fighting that there were almost none to be had; the whole notion of a horse club seemed not just ludicrously extravagant but genuinely immoral. At the same time, the club was a place where younger members of the prewar aristocratic and moneyed elites, whose status and fortunes were rapidly declining, could give vent in the most vivacious manner to their rebelliousness, their despair, their escapism. It was a place where men and women who had taken advantage of the defeat to line their own pockets—the up-and-coming masters of toadying and cozying up to the occupiers—could begin to taste what it was like to move up in the world, to be victorious. Every so often an American military family came to the riding grounds, too, or joined in longer rides, having been invited by such Japanese.

There was a woman, the widow of a soldier who had died in the war, who knew how to speak English quite well and thus served as a point of contact with the occupation and generally gadded about with the foreigners. She was called Mrs. Kitao, and she was often at the club. A rumor started going around that Kizaki had gotten involved with this flashy widow, and some busybody talked to Ineko's mother. She didn't actually believe it, but it occurred to her that having her husband take Ineko along to the club would allow her to keep an eye out and prevent anything from happening. Kizaki didn't hesitate a bit; far from it. He was thrilled. Ineko, with her five-year-old-girl instincts, took an immediate dislike to Mrs. Kitao. And she saw that her father disliked the widow, too. As a former army officer, the fierce pain of the defeat and the ruins around him continued to rankle; his prosthetic right leg and the aching nerves in the stump were a constant reminder—or perhaps a consolation. He was in no state to be making eyes at such a woman. For her part, Mrs. Kitao was just learning to ride, though sticking a little too close to her teacher.

The first time little Ineko mounted a horse, she sat pressed against her father's stomach while he cradled her in his arm. She grew to like horses, and learned to ride alone. All through her childhood, people thought of her as the club's mascot. Her father looked on her as more than just his greatest treasure; she was the very source of his life. And he loved more than anything to see his young daughter on horseback. He didn't just take her to the club; he let her come along on the excursions, too. Ineko was happy. Her father took pride in her, and she felt proud of him. But Kizaki, who had always hated losing, began on account of his missing leg to shy less and less from danger, both at the club and on excursions. Ineko saw only what a magnificent rider he was.

"I felt so awful it was like the blood had frozen in my veins. I still do," Ineko's mother said, continuing her story. "I know I killed him, I did—by giving in to the jealousy we women feel, the suspicions. If I hadn't told him to take our little Ineko to the club she would never have started riding, and he would never had gone on that trip with her."

"Ah?" Kuno didn't quite know what to say to this.

"Well it's true, isn't it?" the mother said, her tone full of self-reproach. "I wanted to die, too ... not a double suicide, that's not it—to follow him in death. If it hadn't been for Ineko, I would have. To atone for my sins, in part."

"Hold on."

"What?"

"You're suggesting that if you hadn't been jealous, if you hadn't let Ineko learn to ride, then the accident that killed your husband would never have happened?"

"That's right."

"How strange."

"It's not strange at all."

"No, that's not what I mean. It feels sort of like we've just switched places, the way you're talking to me now, and how I was talking to you before." Kuno thought for a moment. "I wonder if people all think alike at these times, in these extreme circumstances."

"You think so?" Ineko's mother said. Kuno's remark seemed to have her caught off guard. "I don't know about that, but ... I think my wanting to die after Kizaki's accident and your wanting to marry Ineko even though she has lost her mind are two entirely different things. I would feel terrible for Ineko if they aren't."

"No, no, they are different. I'm not saying I want to marry her because she's been diagnosed with somagnosia—we decided to marry before. I just haven't changed my mind."

"I know. But now you feel sorry for her."

"Yes, pity is part of it now, too. But let's not talk about that."

"I'm sorry."

"You could say compassion has deepened my feelings for her. But I really just want to stay with her, to be with her constantly and help her recover."

"I understand that," the mother said simply.

Kuno looked at her. "Have you ever told Ineko how you feel about her father's accident, Mother? That maybe ultimately your jealousy was to blame?"

"Ineko felt that way before I did. She was obsessed with the thought that it was her fault, her responsibility—that she had killed her father. It's only natural. After all, it happened right in front of her. They were galloping along side by side when he tumbled off the cliff into the ocean. And she was just a girl, at the most sensitive age. It's enough to drive anyone mad."

"Ah."

"That's partly why I told her about that pathetic jealously of mine—to calm her, to loosen the knot in her heart."

The mother's feet slowed as she walked the narrow path, and for a moment it seemed she might stumble into the grass along the bank. Kuno put a hand lightly on her shoulder.

"A woman must never be jealous, Ineko—you must never doubt a man. In the end, that's what I told her. She was choked with tears at the time, sobbing at her father's death, but then just like that she stopped, stunned, and stared at me." The mother looked as if her eyes were hurting her. "I'm sure my words must have struck a chord, given the timing, given how she was feeling, and now she'll never forget them. If she ever does get better, Mr. Kuno, and you marry her, I can promise you she won't ever be jealous. She'll never doubt you, Mr. Kuno."

"That's awful."

"Yes, it is. I felt bad later, having said such a thing, but by then it was too late. There's no way for me to take it back now."

"So Ineko will never be jealous. She'll never doubt me!" All of a sudden, Kuno burst out laughing. His tone was cheerful, as if he were trying to persuade himself that Ineko's mother had been joking. "No, she'll be jealous. She sulks in the most adorable way. For instance ... here, I'll give you an example. You know those very tightly rolled cigarettes? The ones you've got to soften a bit in your palm first, before you light them? So I was squeezing one of those stiff cigarettes one day, and Ineko lit a match. And here's what she says— it's great. She says, 'I'm sure the girls in bars are always ready with a match. You were thinking of one just now, weren't you. I can tell.'"

"Please," the mother muttered, unimpressed.

"One more. Back when I was sitting for my graduation exams, this girl I knew lent me her notes for two of the subjects, so I danced with her more than anyone else at the graduation party. When I told Ineko that story, she asked, 'And what was she wearing, this girl? A kimono or a dress? Did the dress have an open back?' I suppose she was imagining my hand on the girl's skin while we danced, if the dress were backless. It was a shock to realize how sensitive young women are about these things. 'And how was her handwriting? Was it neat? Pretty? Maybe I should take some lessons to improve my penmanship.' Isn't that adorable?"

"Please don't confuse the issue, Mr. Kuno. These childish anecdotes won't distract me," the mother said. "You don't really believe a woman's jealousy is as silly as all that?"

"............"

"You don't, do you?"

"But—"

"*But* what? Ineko and I both detest that word. It would be nice if you could avoid using 'but' in conversation with her."

"Yes, but ... listen Mother. The conjunction *but* lets us change our thoughts, steer them in a fresh direction—it's how we humans rescue ourselves from the anxieties that entrap us, and open new paths forward. I couldn't survive in any place, be it paradise or hell, where the use of *but* was forbidden."

"All right. *But* ... what?"

"Okay, let's think hypothetically a moment. Whenever Ineko sees a horse, she goes pale and her body starts shaking. And yet she can still ride a horse if she tries. I've never had riding lessons. But I can at least stay on a horse. Ineko would find it horrible to return to the cliff where her father fell and died, there's no question about that. But as long as that road in Izu exists, as long there are horses in the world and she and I are still alive, there's always a possibility that she and I might one day get up on our horses and ride down that road."

"What are you trying to say? I don't understand."

"That's how *but* works. It's an example."

"Ah, I see." The mother nodded, then continued: "So you're thinking of taking Ineko to that spot, having her ride past it with you, the two of you, as a way of healing the pain and the sorrow she still carries in her heart from her father's death—is that the idea? I think I've heard of neurologists or psychiatrists or some sort of doctor using a method like that."

"It makes sense. I suppose it could happen, especially if Ineko and I were married, living happily together, and we made a trip to Izu to pray for her father's spirit … Well, she might have a sort of catharsis," Kuno said calmly. "And if, on that cliff, her father's spirit should call and Ineko herself, on her horse, should tumble into the ocean, I would go down with her. I think I would be happy with that."

"Stop it, Mr. Kuno. Her father's spirit isn't vengeful, that I can say for sure," the mother said emphatically. "If the cliff should crumble beneath her, her father's spirit would lift Ineko up, hold her aloft in space, so she could live. I'm convinced of that. The dead protect the living. Ineko's father isn't in a grave, or enshrined in an altar, but he is there inside her, within Ineko—clearly, strongly there. He's inside me, too."

"Mother," Kuno said. "The trip to Izu, that was just an example."

"You can go riding there if you like, if it will make Ineko better."

"What you said before was very sad—that Ineko could never be jealous, never doubt me. And now I'm wondering whether that might have been it. Maybe something made her jealous, suspicious, and suppressing it took so much effort that it drove her crazy."

"Some trifle like your friend in the backless dress?"

"No. Something I never even noticed, but that was very hurtful to her—that's what I'm asking myself. That's the sort of sickness so-magnosia seems to be, right? An effort not to see a part of yourself, of a loved one, of life. A blindness that stems for some deep wound."

"You understand her that much?"

"That much even I can see," Kuno said. "But you know, Mother, I brought up that idea of riding in Izu just as an example, but I wonder … is it better to let her rest in the asylum with her eyes closed, waiting until the film that clouds her vision falls away on its own, or to let her marry me and then make her open them, by force if need be? Have you really thought about that, in a serious way? Are you afraid to take that risk?"

"Don't you remember what I said, Mr. Kuno? Will you really be content if she can't see you when you lie together? Wouldn't that disturb you?"

"It's fine. I told you before. So she can't see me; she'll feel me touching her."

"There you go again." Once more, the mother blushed slightly. "Have you considered how awful that would be for Ineko? All that matters is how it is for you?"

"Now that's ridiculous." Kuno gazed at the mother, his gaze more pitying than anything else. "How could any man say such a thing?"

"Men have that side to them, I think."

"Do they? Because they're not as sensitive as women, I suppose?"

"Being ill isn't the same as being sensitive."

"Clearly you think it was her sensitivity that brought the illness on. Maybe it did, I don't know. But either way, is tossing a sensitive person into a madhouse a sensitive treatment?"

"Please don't, Mr. Kuno." Ineko's mother grimaced. "I took our doctor's advice. Doctors know about sickness."

"Doctors. Doctors, too, for diseases of the heart. Like they know anything."

"Ikuta Clinic seems like a nice place. Warm, peaceful."

Kuno looked back at the hill where the clinic stood, hidden by trees.

"You can still hear Ineko's bell. The ringing seems regular enough, even if it's a lunatic striking it. You can hear the sound flying through the sky, over the town, flowing out to sea. Seeing us down the road."

"Ineko isn't a lunatic now, Mr. Kuno. Not when she's striking the bell."

"No, I know. I wonder how long she plans to keep on with it, though? Maybe the nurse makes her go on striking it? Or can she decide to stop on her own? If she pushes herself too hard, she might stop seeing the bell. From her somagnosia, I mean."

"A bell isn't a body."

"Ah." Kuno nodded, then murmured, as if to himself, "A bell is not a person. Kizaki's horse wasn't a person, either. And yet when these things are connected to someone in an extreme state, they become people. Isn't that right, Mother?"

"Let's not talk about horses anymore."

"You realize, Mother, that you and Ineko may have been on completely the wrong track with this fatalistic, karmic-retribution-style idea you've been beating yourselves up with, about the horses. That you might just be thinking too much. That's the sense I got, listening to you. The way you see it, right, you had little Ineko's father take her to the riding club because you were jealous, suspicious, and if you hadn't then Ineko would never have learned to ride. If she hadn't become a rider, she and her father wouldn't have taken that trip to Izu. And without that trip, Father never would have had his accident. So in the end, your jealousy was the cause that resulted in Father's death."

"Yes."

"That's a pretty conceited sense of fate, if you ask me. A very self-centered take on karma, or destiny, if you prefer. You flatter yourself with an enlightenment you don't possess."

"What a thing to say!"

"If that's really how you see things, Mother, then shouldn't you blame the very fact that you and Father were born in the same age? And that life brought the two of you together? Worst of all, of course, was your marriage to him, and that you gave birth to a baby girl named Ineko. Isn't that right? All that together is what caused Father's accident—in a distant way, yes, but still. If you follow the chain of your regrets to the end, that's where you end up. What a stupid way to think about fate. Okay, maybe it's not stupid, I don't know. But your regrets certainly are. There's no end to it, once you start feeling bad about things in the past. You can't even stop with your own generation. It was your parents' fault for giving birth to a woman like you, and it was ... so it goes, on and on. Before you know it, you'll end up laying the responsibility on the very existence of the human race."

"Are you trying to bully me?" Ineko's mother asked bluntly, though she had plainly been shaken by Kuno's agitated tone. "Or did you mean all that to be comforting?"

"I don't know that it's comforting ... at any rate, I didn't mean to hurt you," Kuno said. "It's another *but*, actually. I just wanted to point out that there's another way of looking at it—precisely the opposite of yours. Can't you look at it like this instead? If Ineko hadn't started visiting the riding club with her father, if she hadn't learned to ride, and if they never went on that trip together, Father might well have died sooner still, before the accident even had a chance to happen?"

"What!"

"After all, Ineko was his joy, his happiness, perhaps even the source of his life. For all we know, she might have given him more time to live. Not even the gods of destiny could say for certain that that wasn't the case."

"It's all a matter of perspective, I suppose." Ineko's mother uttered this platitude in the most commonplace tone she could manage, but she had a look on her face as if she'd spotted an unexpected patch of blue in a cloudy sky. It was possible to think of things the way Kuno had said. At the very least, it was true that Ineko's father had been happy watching his daughter learn to ride, and traveling with her on horseback. The young Ineko wasn't the only one who was happy then.

"All a matter of perspective? That's just the kind of careless, evasive response that—" Kuno paused a moment, then continued, "I don't like. It irritates me."

"Because you're young, Mr. Kuno." Once again the mother replied with a platitude, and in the same platitudinous tone. She didn't necessarily mean to hide her feelings, but it struck her as she spoke that her comments might have kept Kuno from noticing that bit of sunshine in her heart. "Isn't that what saves us? The idea that it's all perspective?"

"Well, yes, I guess you could say that religion, philosophy, and morality are all rooted in perspective," Kuno said. "But the way you used the phrase just now, that was simply a trick, a clever attempt to avoid having to formulate an actual perspective. Saying I'm young, too ... that's just one of those slimy things old people say. Thinking like that leads nowhere. To be frank, it isn't really thinking at all. That sort of 'perspective' is where people end up when they've thought so long and so hard that they just don't know what to think anymore."

"I see no reason I should have to listen to you scolding me like this, Mr. Kuno," said the mother. Something close to a smile was playing on her face, though—an outward sign that the tightness in her chest had loosened. "Hearing you before, those things you said, I saw that there *was* another way of looking at things that could give us, Ineko and me, some comfort. I really mean that. When you've been hammered down by something awful, it's easy to think you have no choice but to keep walking down the same road, looking neither right nor left, your hair as disheveled as your thoughts, with the echoes of that awful event coming after you, or dragging you forward, since either way it's *their* road. That's how it has been for Ineko and me. But it seems maybe there are times when, just like that, you can turn off onto a side street."

"There you go again," Kuno said sternly. "I never said anything about going off onto some side street. I wasn't talking about that sort of slapdash 'perspective' at all."

Ineko's mother nodded. "I understand that. I'm grateful for what you've said. But people are creatures of inventive self-justification, of self-affirmation. I don't believe animals do that sort of thing. They don't have language, after all. Or maybe they do, maybe animals are pure bundles of self-affirmation, but it's beautiful for them, because it's instinctual, and because they lack the words for justifying themselves."

"You're not making any effort to understand what I said. Would understanding me somehow violate your conscience? I'm not trying to offer you an excuse, a way out. I'm not trying to help you out by thinking through destiny inside out."

"I know that. Didn't I just say I took comfort in your perspective?"

Kuno walked two or three steps, not exactly watching Ineko's mother, but keeping silent in a way that suggested he was conscious of her.

"I haven't heard Ineko's bell in a while," he said. "Have you?"

"Oh? I guess not." The mother looked back at the hill where the Ikuta Clinic stood.

Kuno turned back, too. "She must have stopped ringing it."

"You think so?"

"Maybe she was tired."

"Or the nurse made her stop. I'm sure the townspeople would be annoyed if they kept ringing the bell for ages when it's only three o'clock."

The trees on the low hill, surrounding the clinic and Jōkōji, were dense evergreens, mostly broadleaves, with the deep green, almost black hue typical of warmer regions. The richness of their coloring made it seem as if they could have been growing there untended for a millennium, as if the hill were perhaps an ancient imperial burial mound. The grave-like mood came from the stillness of the place, of course; it wasn't at all dark. The sky above the trees looked wintry in some subtle way, shaded by the shortness of the days. A flock of six or seven birds rose up at an angle from behind the trees, from left to right, and began flying toward town. The mother found it odd to see them approaching in silence, but she didn't mention it to Kuno.

It was after three now, in winter, and dusk was approaching. How did the mad behave at sundown? Did they become wilder? The mother didn't know, but the thought worried her. She had only just left her daughter at the clinic.

"You know, Mother," Kuno said, "I've said the same thing to Ineko, too, of course, once before. And with more passion than I said it just now. I said that her riding gave her father joy, that it made him happy, that it was the source of his life."

"What did Ineko say?"

"And she helped him, a defeated solider, hang on to his life. I'm sure you can see where this is going, though. She was very upset that I had described her father as defeated."

"Yes, she would be. That's the kind of person she is."

"She was very sharp with me. *You didn't see my father fall from the cliff and die, Mr. Kuno*, she said. I told her the image had been imprinted on my heart, burned there, ever since she'd told me the story, because that was the core of a tragedy in the life of the woman I loved. Maybe I could actually see it more clearly, I said, because she had been too panicked to look, whereas I was able to call on deep reserves of sympathy to imagine the scene. She didn't accept that, though. She thought it was nonsense."

The flock of birds flew overhead on its way to the shore, so low that Kuno and Ineko's mother could hear the beating of their wings. Neither looked up, however.

"I've never known what to believe," the mother said. "When you hear her tell the story, it seems so strange that she could have seen it all so clearly. I almost think it must have been a hallucination that came out of her terror. I can't say how many times I've asked her about it. Maybe you saw it in a dream? You had a nightmare, and then convinced yourself that that was reality? Because the truth is she fainted, you know, the moment Kizaki fell over the cliff."

Ineko had lost consciousness while she was still riding her horse. She was such a practiced rider that even then she didn't tumble off. She kept a firm grip on the reins. The two horses had been galloping full speed, side by side, but when it happened Ineko's slowed—not because she had reined it in, but because the horse itself sensed that it should. If Ineko hadn't fainted, she might well have thrown herself off the cliff after her father.

Ineko hadn't witnessed the moment when her father's horse, galloping on the side of the road nearer the ocean, slipped.

By the time she screamed and closed her eyes, her father and his horse were already plummeting from that high cliff into the ocean. Her father was clinging with both arms to his horse's neck. The horse writhed, pumping its feet in the air. The cliff's wall was sheer but rough, studded with boulders, and midway down a giant shelf of rock jutted out into the air. Ineko couldn't hear the crash of the bodies hitting the rock, of course, but she felt it—the pain blasting into her body as man and horse were separated. The horse dropped first, stomach turned to the sky, his neck curling like a bow toward his belly. The man, her father, was falling lengthwise and twisted so that his head faced down, and just then his prosthetic leg parted from his torso. Ineko felt it happening. Most likely it had been detached when his body hit the rock shelf. Either way, when she looked back on her feelings at that terrible moment—it wasn't that she couldn't explain it, that wasn't the point—the leg filled her with horror. Her father's left leg was sticking straight out. Inside his riding breeches, it had already parted from the human—it was death.

A splash rose high from the azure ocean. The human sank. The horse flailed in the water for a moment, struggling to swim, then stopped moving. Ineko fainted.

That was how Ineko's father had died, as Ineko told the story. There was ample room to question, as the mother did, whether Ineko had actually seen these things, but Ineko believed she had. Ineko had no idea why the horse had floated when it hit the water, while the human disappeared from view. She couldn't even be sure her father had sunk for good. He might have gone under only to bob up again—she wouldn't have seen him, she was unconscious by then.

"It's only to be expected that a young woman would faint after such a terrible shock, but if fainting kept her alive, then perhaps you could say it was fate, too, stepping in to help. That moment of unconsciousness," Kuno said. "Divine protection, as they say."

"Divine protection?" Ineko's mother repeated. "That sounds like something people used to say all the time, but don't anymore. In any event, you're talking about God, I assume? You don't strike me, Mr. Kuno, as someone likely believe in God."

"Call it fate, then."

"You believe in fate?"

"Sometimes events compel you to see them in those terms, whether or not you believe. I don't deny that it's trite and banal to marvel at fate after a brush with something awful when you don't generally give it a second thought, but still, I can't help wondering whether Ineko would even be alive today if she hadn't lost consciousness."

"Her father's fate was much worse, going over that cliff." Once again, the mother's gaze clouded. "If Ineko hadn't actually fainted, if she had just gone into an indiscriminate frenzy, becoming so distraught that she plunged off the cliff with her horse—even then her death would have seemed like a side effect, or maybe an aftereffect, of her father's fate."

"How can you say that?" Kuno snapped, so vehemently Ineko's mother was taken aback. "I wasn't talking about her father. I'm not talking about anyone who isn't here, who isn't part of this life we're living. I never met Ineko's father, never talked to him. You know that. When it occurred to me that Ineko's riding as a girl was a comfort to her father, that it might have helped him survive the defeat, and when I said as much to Ineko and you, I was thinking of the two of you, of course—of the living. I didn't say it for her father, who's dead anyway."

"Yes, I know that. Didn't I thank you earlier, Mr. Kuno, for showing us a different way to look at things? It's a matter of perspective, I said. You remember."

"I'm not happy with that. As I said before, I wasn't trying to do you a favor by finding some way to turn the meaning of her father's death, his fate, inside out—to open a patch of light in the mass of clouds that hangs over those he left behind," Mr. Kuno continued. "I'm sure you'd agree, wouldn't you, that when someone dies, the family and friends usually try to hide their regret and self-recrimination, their pangs of conscience, behind a mask of grief and loss that only they, the living, can wear? The living have no power over death, be it from sickness or accident. Murder is the exception, of course. But even then, it seems to me there must be something in the victim's fate that calls it on, something more than just the broken destiny of the killer, since murder isn't in our nature, or in our instincts. I may be young, but I've seen a fair number of people die, people I was close to, and as a result of that, I suppose, I've come to think there's something insolent in mourning the dead, tying death to oneself in that way. However lovingly you tend to someone, if he's going to die, he dies. If that's his fate, if the god of death has put its hand on him, then nothing he can do, nothing anyone who loves him can do, no matter how deep their love may be, will save him. Perhaps its true that 'destiny' and 'the god of death' and so on are just words primitive people used to name their fears and their sense of wonderment, but once a word is created, all sorts of things and stories emerge to give it form. The god of death assumes various guises and figures in any number of stories—and people didn't think of those as visions or dreams. In their eyes, the god of death was real. You know, every once in a while, I wonder how the ancients, people who lived before the word *fate* was born, before the characters we use to write it existed, how they felt about these things—man's destiny, death. I have studied these things very little, so it's just me thinking, musing. Not that possessing that sort of knowledge or doing that research would actually enable anyone living in a later age to fathom the hearts of the ancients." Kuno paused. "It's shallow and pointless, Mother, I know. All I'm trying to say is that I don't think you and Ineko will go on living in the shadow of Kizaki's death forever, and that I hope one day you'll make your way out into the sun, into the light of life. You were your husband's wife and Ineko was her father's daughter, it's true, but when he went over that cliff, that was his fate and his alone. I genuinely believe that."

"But Ineko was there with him, Mr. Kuno. She witnessed it, as his daughter. Surely you'll agree there's no way she can escape from that."

"Yes," Kuno said clearly, "but her father fell and died—and she fainted and lived."

"That's a terrible thing to say."

"It happens all the time with fatal accidents. Two soldiers are crouching together when one gets hit by a bullet and dies. Someone is killed in a car crash, and the person in the next seat goes home without a scratch. Those are just some easy examples. You can say the same thing about sickness, too—say you have a husband and wife who have been married for forty years, and he's diagnosed with cancer. She can't get cancer with him, even if she wants to."

A smile drifted across the mother's face. "Well, this isn't like that, is it? If Ineko had kept an eye on the ground, watching where her father's horse was going, he wouldn't have fallen off the cliff—her inattention killed him. That's how she sees it, and that's why she has been suffering all this time. The notion that she would have flung herself into the ocean after him if she hadn't fainted seems a bit fantastic—just the kind of idea that might occur to a girl in the frenzy of such a moment."

"If Ineko had jumped that day, I would never have met her. She would never have come into my life." Kuno was silent for a moment. "And what about you, Mother? If they had both died that day. The life you have lived from then until this day."

"Let's not talk about Kizaki's death anymore, Mr. Kuno."

"I just think you and Ineko are too hung up on his death, after all this time. It's fine to miss him, to feel sad, but nursing the sort of regret you do, punishing yourselves for what happened—it's disrespectful to the gods of destiny. It's like you've slammed the gate on your lives, shut yourself up in the dark. That's why I said those things. I just went on too long."

"No. You're welcome to go on and on about it as much as you like. After all, though his death certainly pained me, it left a much deeper wound in Ineko's heart." The mother looked at Kuno, not quite directly and not quite with upturned eyes, but in a manner that was somehow both simultaneously. "I've been wanting to ask you for some time now, Mr. Kuno—do you think Ineko's somagnosia is related to her witnessing her father's death? Could that be what caused it? Have you ever noticed anything along those lines, or had some reason to wonder? When she told you how he died, for instance, or on some other occasion?"

"It's hard to say." Kuno cocked his head, thinking. His face took on a look of just barely concealed distress. "No, I don't think it's that. Of course, psychology isn't my field."

"To tell the truth, I don't believe there's any causal relationship between Ineko's father's death and this sickness, either, and I'd prefer to think there isn't. I only asked because you mentioned it. His death, I mean."

"That's not true—you're the one who brought it up. And I only talked like that to try and release you from the dark weight of that story. I didn't say anything about the death itself."

"I know," the mother said simply. "Please, let's stop talking about it."

"I agree. You know, I might have said something along those lines, about her somagnosia having something to do with her father's accident. But I don't really think it does. I just wondered whether, somewhere in all that, there might be a cure for her disease. It's odd, isn't it? Even though I don't believe the first misfortune triggered the second. Even though I don't think the two are related."

"Somehow people tend to feel that all misfortunes are connected."

"Do they? I don't see it that way," Kuno said. "But if you do, Mother, if you genuinely do, then wasn't putting Ineko in the madhouse a mistake? Doesn't it just add another block to the pile of misfortune, thread another bead on the rosary?"

"I wonder. I consider Ineko very fortunate to have been loved by a man like you, and I think she's lucky we were able to find a place like the Ikuta Clinic."

"Nice as the clinic may be, I'd discharge her tomorrow if I could," Kuno said forcefully. "Mother, please, go back with me tomorrow morning. We can stay in Ikuta tonight."

"You have trouble letting go, don't you, Mr. Kuno. More than me, though I'm a woman, and her mother," Ineko's mother said. "All right, though, I'm willing to spend the night in town and go up in the morning to see how she's doing. But you agreed at the beginning that we should put her in the clinic, so this business about taking her out ... no."

"I never wanted to put her in an asylum. You know that. I asked you for her hand."

"To let you marry my mad daughter? My somagnosic Ineko?"

"Sometimes she can't see people's bodies. So what? Does something like that even count as a mental illness?" Kuno asked. Then, blushing, and lowering his voice as if it embarrassed him to go on: "Doesn't that happen with women occasionally, that they stop seeing the person they're with at the most intense moment of their loving? I'm too much of a neophyte, I lack both the experience and the knowledge to say such a thing. You've lived your whole life as a woman, though."

"My husband was a soldier, Mr. Kuno, blunt and unpolished," the mother replied. "I may never have known the sort of womanly happiness to which you refer."

"I don't think that's relevant, being a solider or not. Besides, what about other women? Don't you hear about these things from them?"

"The women I associate with tend to be quite proper, I'm afraid. I've never had the sort of friends who would openly discuss such secretive … well, secrets," the mother said. "And in any event—I don't mean to suggest you're giving yourself too much credit, though I know that's how this will sound—you weren't the first to experience Ineko's somagnosia. If you'd been the only one, we wouldn't have had to commit her. Married couples can accommodate all kinds of peculiar things. Sooner or later, it seems, something unusual will crop up between even the most ordinary of men and women. And that's all right, whatever it may be, as long as they themselves don't mind. If it becomes intolerable, there's always the option of divorce. I suppose if you're going to have a secret, though, it's best if it's unique, not like the secrets other couples share. At any rate, Ineko's troubles went beyond that, as you know."

Kuno was silent. He was reflecting on his own responsibility for Ineko's disease.

"We'll do as you suggest—stay in Ikuta tonight, then go back to the clinic tomorrow," the mother said. "I'm sure we'll be able to get a room someplace."

"Every town has a place to stay. Besides, the train stops here. It's only one night, I'm sure you can put up with one of those inns salespeople stay in, even a dirty travel lodge."

Ineko's mother nodded. "Of course, I'll be fine."

They would probably have the best shot at finding an inn if they crossed the small bridge downstream and went into town, to the area around the station. Already, the sand at the river's mouth had taken on the colors of a winter evening. Those birds that had flown noiselessly overhead were nowhere to be seen now, and the faint gray horizon was shrouded by a vague, madder red haze. Whether the sky had bled downward or the placid sea had risen was unclear; either way, there was no border. The meager flow of the river emptying into the ocean, too, was a dull color.

Ineko's mother was just stepping onto the small earthen bridge that led into town when she gasped. A boy who recalled the brilliant, deep yellow of a dandelion had scampered past. She turned to watch as he ran off. So did Kuno.

"Was that a human boy?" Ineko's mother murmured, seemingly to herself.

"What do you mean, Mother?" Kuno said, startled.

"Could there be fairies in this town? Did you see his face?"

"Don't be absurd. He had on an ordinary elementary school uniform, shoes and all. He looked perfectly normal."

"I'd like to steal him and take him home," the mother said, staring after him as he ran off upstream. "I guess that would mean I'd kidnapped him."

"It would. I doubt you could kidnap a boy his age anyway. He looked sharp."

"How about adopting him?"

"Maybe you could do that." Kuno gazed at her, puzzled. "What's gotten into you, all of a sudden? You have Ineko. She and I can live with you, even after we're married."

"I felt lonely, all of a sudden. I think that boy must have been a spirit of the river or the ocean or something who came to plant that loneliness in me and then ran off."

This made no sense to Kuno, but it didn't seem worth pursuing. She would feel better in the morning, he assumed, after she got some sleep. He thought of the boy's eyes looking out under those lovely eyebrows, seeming to absorb everything; his innocent lips, which looked as if they could brush away a life of suffering and disease with a single touch; the voice that, he felt sure, with all the beauty of a hymn would burrow into your heart.

Still, that Ineko's mother should be drawn so forcefully to the boy after glimpsing him on the bank hinted at a loneliness in her, a sorrow, beyond words. The thought pained him. For the first time, he realized that the intensity of his concern for Ineko had prevented him from paying much attention to her mother. He'd only been thinking of her as she related to Ineko.

"I don't care if he *was* a fairy. There are lots of old stories about people living with fairies, but nowadays you're lucky if you can meet one on the street. You really saw him, Mr. Kuno?"

"Of course. He was just a boy, in primary school, maybe his first year in middle school," Kuno said. The thought occurred to him that maybe she had some mental issues of her own, just like Ineko.

"You like pretty boys, Mother, is that it?" he teased.

"Hardly." The mother grimaced. "I've always disliked children, boys and girls. Even their smell gets to me."

"At his age he might not have that sort of scent."

"That's beside the point. He was a fairy. Fairies have hands and feet just like anyone else. I'm surprised you saw him, actually. If only Ineko could see him—I bet he'd cure her."

"Maybe that's why I saw him, then—we're connected."

"You didn't find him otherworldly?"

"The same question again. He was beautiful, but he was a human child. Would you like me to chase after him and call him back?"

Ineko's mother shook her head. "I don't suppose he could have been on his way home after visiting someone at the Ikuta Clinic."

"Surely not." Kuno looked disbelievingly at Ineko's mother. "He's a local. Towns like this always have one or two unusually beautiful children."

"Why is that?"

"I have no idea. Some odd effect of having old families around, maybe."

"Not fairies?"

"Not fairies. Though if you think that's what they are, perhaps that's the truth."

"It's a small town, Mr. Kuno. I can ask at the inn if they know him, once we find one." The mother was still unwilling to give up. "I bet if I did, they'd just frown and say he didn't sound familiar."

"Meaning your theory is right—he really was a spirit of the river or the ocean? Next time I see him, I'll grab him for you, I promise. I'm not sure you can even grab a fairy, but at least it won't count as kidnapping the way it would with a human boy. I must say, though, Mother—you sure come out with some peculiar things. Not only is he a fairy, but he can cure Ineko."

"You have until tomorrow morning, then."

"Impossible. I don't even know where he lives."

"That's true. And if he is a fairy, maybe we're the only ones who see him—maybe Ineko's sprightly side has imbued us with the power to see him. It would be nice if we could take him with us tomorrow morning, though, when we go to see her at the clinic."

"I said that's impossible," Kuno said, an irritated note in his voice. "Anyway, just what sort of effect do you expect him to have on her?"

"I like the atmosphere at the Ikuta Clinic, I really do. But more than trees and grass, more than the sky and the soil, I think a sort of fairy in human form—a heart so perfect in its innocence that it goes beyond what we usually mean by innocence—might assuage the spasms of the mad, in ways we can't even comprehend. It's just a thought that occurred to me. You and I know Ineko so well that we're no help. But she's never met that boy, so maybe ... just like that ..."

"You talk like he's an angel, or a medium."

"Exactly. I think the world even now is full of people who might as well be angels. And they can wipe away a mental illness just like that, especially a mild case."

"Perhaps you're right." Kuno frowned. "We don't want to leave everything to her doctor. We can discuss it at the inn tonight. If any other miraculous cures come to mind as we talk, we can talk about them as well."

The two stepped from the bank of the river onto the earthen bridge. It wasn't large enough to have a handrail. The grass at either end was a pristine green, not a speck of dust on the blades, a color so deep it was hard to believe it was February; this green, too, seemed to express the life of this town. Dandelions grew among the weeds. Their leaves spread wide and low, thrusting aside the hardy growth around them. Full of vitality, and large for dandelions, they radiated in all directions. You wondered, seeing them, whether the dandelions in this region were stronger, more determined to live, than those elsewhere. They were all already producing buds; some had bloomed, with three or even four flowers. These flowers, too, were large for dandelions, the petals uncommonly thick, their yellow unusually deep.

"Dandelions close up in the evening and open again in the morning, don't they? Does that sound right to you?" Ineko's mother asked.

"Really?" Kuno stared at the flowers. "I have no idea—I've never heard that before. You hardly see any dandelions in Tokyo these days, but even if I did, I wouldn't look at one closely enough to notice when it closes and opens."

"Yes, people are surprisingly oblivious when it comes to such things. And dandelions are wildflowers, no one really cares. I've never heard of anyone growing them, not in fields, not even in pots. But then I was raised in the countryside. I can't even recall when I first noticed, or learned—it just came to me now that dandelions are like that. That they close up in the evening and open in the morning. A childhood memory, I suppose, not even a memory. But in fact I'm not at all sure that it's true."

"Now that you mention it, Mother, look at that big one there." Kuno pointed. "Doesn't it look like its petals are starting to close? Don't the tips arch out more during the day, around the rim, when they're fully open?"

"Perhaps." Ineko's mother replied, almost inaudibly.

"Because it's almost dusk, I suppose. Out on the ocean, too, and in the sky," Kuno said. "The clinic bell will ring again at six. Then at nine, if I remember right. Ineko won't necessarily be ringing it. Though perhaps it will sound to us as though she is."

"The bell?"

"I imagine we'll be having dinner at the inn when the six-o'clock bell rings. By nine, we may already have gone to bed. I doubt there would be anything to do even if we stayed up in a town like this. Of course, we won't yet have fallen asleep."

"I don't want to hear the clinic bell anymore," Ineko's mother replied vacantly.

"You must be exhausted, taking Ineko up to the clinic, leaving her there," Kuno said, gazing at Ineko's mother's face. "Perhaps it would be best if you went right to bed, as soon as we've found an inn."

"I doubt I could get to sleep."

The bridge was hardly long enough to say you had crossed it. No boundary separated the dirt on the bridge from that of the country road; there was no change at all. They walked into town. Nothing in particular caught the eye. This was not the road they had taken up to the clinic, but they were certainly heading toward the station. They saw a few houses with straw roofs. A store on the first floor of one two-story building was selling medicine and cosmetics; the products were neatly arrayed just inside the door, in a space whose dirt floor seemed to have been recently redone. The interior was brightly lit. The little boxes looked unusually bright and colorful.

Pausing to look, they realized that the next building was an inn. The colors in the store seemed to have guided them to the inn. They exchanged glances.

"With a name like Ikuta House, it ought to be one of the better inns in town," Kuno said, "even if it looks pretty run-down." Though Ineko's mother hadn't rebuffed Kuno's repeated suggestion that they stay overnight in town, part of her still felt undecided. And yet when he walked through the door of Ikuta House, she followed.

The two-room suite they were shown into on the second floor—an eight-mat room and a six-mat room—was by no means as shabby as the entryway had led them to expect. The smell of tatami and sake hung in the air. The locals probably used it for parties and so on.

The woman from the inn stepped into the hall and drew back an old, slightly yellowing white curtain. There was the ocean. A few small pines were scattered along the narrow beach. That was it. Compared to the luxuriant, warm-climate green of the trees up on the hill around the Ikuta Clinic, even in February, and to the vivid colors of the river and the grass, the needles on the pines seemed oddly sparse and haggard on the shore. Even their shadows on the sand were blurred, shapeless. The gray ocean, too, wore a forlorn air.

As soon as the woman left, Ineko's mother got up and slid the shōji shut. Only after she had sat down again did she speak. "There don't seem to be any other guests."

"Hard to say. It's not dark yet."

"We get to spend the night in quite a curious place, thanks to you."

"Thanks to me? I thought we were doing this for Ineko."

"Unpleasant to think of being here at night, after it gets dark."

"You're thinking of Ineko? Of what it's like at night up at the clinic?" Kuno asked. "Shall we give her a call to see how she's doing?"

"That won't be necessary, thank you." The mother shook her head.

"We could call the doctor, if you think it's a bad idea to call her."

"That's not necessary."

For reasons Kuno couldn't understand, Ineko's mother looked very stern.

The woman from the inn brought tea and coals for the hibachi.

"We'd like dinner at six," Kuno told her.

"You can close the shutters, too, if you wouldn't mind," the mother added.

"There aren't any shutters, actually," said the woman.

"Really? Just the glass windows and curtains?"

"Yes. The rooms downstairs have them. They're older."

"That's all right, we'll manage."

"Would you like me to bring hot water bottles for your futons, or is a kotatsu preferable?" the woman asked.

"Water bottles are fine," said the mother.

The woman left.

"She didn't say anything either way," Kuno said with a smile, "but I'm guessing that even in a place like this it will be an electric kotatsu. I don't really need either one, honestly—a kotatsu or a hot water bottle."

"Ineko has always had cold feet," the mother murmured pensively. "Maybe she got it from me, I don't know—I remember she did once comment on how cold my feet were. She was an only child, of course, and the sudden death of her father frightened her so much that we slept on the same futon until she got too old for that."

"Ah?"

"It's strange, but some nights her feet were colder than mine, while on others mine were colder—I wonder why."

Kuno remained silent. He couldn't bring himself to speak. Ineko's mother seemed so at ease with him now that she wasn't at all concerned with propriety.

"My late husband once told me he liked it when a woman's hands and feet felt cold at first. Having them warm up as you go along, in other words. Maybe that was because his own body got so hot it was like he was on fire, I'm not sure. Anyway, I've always felt cold. I suppose some men would say they like women to be nice and warm."

"Ah." Oddly enough, it was harder for the young Kuno to parry this sort of remark than it was for the mother, a middle-aged woman, to make it.

"My being so cold doesn't matter, but Ineko worried—she thought maybe it was her fault. Though when we slept together, she'd warm up."

"It's unpleasant just imagining a woman whose body gets so hot," said Kuno blushing.

"I'm sure it's better if a mother's breast is warm, don't you think? When she's feeding her baby?" said the mother.

"My own mother's was warm, I think. Though of course I can't really remember back so far … children create those memories retrospectively, I guess."

"Babies are warm. I think their temperatures are higher than ours."

"Yes." Kuno sounded unsure of himself, and of course he'd never held a baby to his chest to feed it. He'd never been moved enough by touching a baby's skin to remember how high or low its temperature had been.

He knew, though, that Ineko's hands and feet were always cold. He wondered if her mother had been trying to coax him into revealing something by talking in such a seemingly intimate way about the coldness of her own body, and touching so lightly on the coldness of Ineko's limbs. His chest tensed at the thought. Kuno could relax with Ineko's mother, knowing she was as familiar as she could be with him and Ineko, and forgave everything; that was what had made it possible for him to come with her to this place, to deliver Ineko to the Ikuta Clinic. When it came to their relations as man and woman, though, it was only to be expected that much would remain concealed—no matter how openly Ineko spoke with her mother and no matter how much Kuno himself shared. Words could not touch the deepest core of such matters.

The bonds between men and women predate language, and while the words we have used to express those ties may have grown exceptionally subtle and refined since language first arose, they are still just words. Words make our loves richer and more complicated, yes, but much has also been lost on their account—shrouded in the trappings of the age, drunk on the vacuity of artificial thrills. The progress of language is both a friend to love between the sexes and its enemy. Such love abides, it seems, in the mysterious depths where language cannot reach. Perhaps it's a slight exaggeration to say that the language of love is a stimulant, a drug; but whatever led us humans to create such a language, it was not life itself—which is the root of love—and therefore that language cannot engender the life that is the root of all else.

Ineko's somagnosia, too, was beyond language.

Shortly before six, the woman brought dinner in. The grilled fish had cooled, but at least the miso soup was warm.

Ineko's mother had hardly any appetite.

"The rice is undercooked," she said.

Kuno had requested dinner at six because the bell at the clinic would be ringing then. Sure enough, they heard it.

"Did that sound to you like the bell Ineko rang at three, Mother?" Kuno's face clouded. "It's entirely different, right from the first ring."

"Is it?" The mother put down her chopsticks and listened.

"It's just a regular evening bell," Kuno said, "like at any old temple."

"I should think that was obvious," the mother replied.

"And yet the sound fills me with regret," Kuno said, the look on his face so different from a moment ago that he might have been wearing a mask. "Was I wrong, Mother? Have I made a terrible mistake, only I was so wrapped up in my love for Ineko that I didn't notice? That bell—it's as if it's sucking the life from my heart, dragging me down into a darkness that never ends. Who's striking it now, I wonder? A madman in the throes of some evil passion, a noble confessor? How many times will it ring? Let me listen in silence, please. You, too—listen."

"It's just a bell at a mountain temple, that's all." Ineko's mother glanced, puzzled, at Kuno's face, more interested in his demeanor than in the bell. She was discreet enough that he may not have realized she was observing him; maybe he thought she was concentrating on the bell, as he had suggested. She kept silent for a few moments, saying nothing to disabuse him.

"A moment ago, Mr. Kuno," she said at last, "you said it sounded like any other evening bell. How, after two or three rings, ten or fifteen seconds, did it come to sound so awful?"

"Awful isn't the word, I think," Kuno said, as if to himself. "When I said all that just now about the madman obsessed with evil, the noble confessor; about being dragged into the darkness … it felt like some sixth sense had suddenly stirred inside me."

"A madman obsessed with evil … ? A confessor … ? I'm afraid there's no way I'll ever understand some of these things you're saying to me, Mr. Kuno."

"Let me listen in silence. Isn't that what I asked?"

Ineko's mother nodded, then slid the shōji open and stepped out into the hall, closing the shōji behind her. She lifted the edge of the old, dingy curtain and stood gazing out at the sea. At a little after six on a winter evening, there was nothing to look at. No light shining from the lighthouse on the island. No moon in the sky. The horizon was lost in the light mist that hung over the water. Even the gray waves racing blandly up the beach were invisible unless you were actively trying to spot them. The small pines on the beach, too, were unremarkable. Though perhaps the plainness of the evening shore suited this quiet, peaceful, aging town.

While there was nothing to catch the eye on the beach or out on the ocean, the sky above was full of stars, though the mist dulled them. You couldn't help imagining how clear the night must be above the haze. To Ineko's mother, it sounded as though the tolling of the bell was ascending into the starry sky, rather than rolling out across the waves. Perhaps that, too, was an effect of the landscape. Still, she heard nothing distinctive in the sound. It hurt to remember the last time they had listened to the bell, at three o'clock, when her own daughter, who they'd just left at the asylum, was striking it. The mother had been thinking about it ever since the ringing started up again at six, of course, but the pain cut deeper as she stood there alone, gazing out at the dark sea and the night. The ordinary ringing of the bell seemed as though it might sound different in a moment. She heard it changing, and assuming the unsteadiness of the bell they'd heard at three, when Ineko was striking it. An auditory hallucination, you might say, that was not a hallucination.

Could it be, then, that Kuno—who started saying those bizarre things about the bell almost right away—loved Ineko more deeply? Returning to the room, the mother quietly sat back down on the floor. Kuno noticed her but said nothing; he seemed to be waiting for the silence between the previous strike of the bell and the next to pass. His expression seemed less stern, though, than it had when she stepped out into the hall.

"I guess that was the last," Kuno said finally. He sighed. "I wonder who it was."

Reassured by the mildness of his tone, the mother replied, "We have no way of knowing, do we? There are any number of patients." Then, as if to soothe him, "You're not still feeling like you did before, are you? That business about the madman, the confessor."

"No." Kuno shook his head.

"That didn't make any sense, Mr. Kuno. What would a confessor be doing in a madhouse? There are doctors—that's all. A prison would have a chaplain, I suppose. But the mad aren't sent to the madhouse to serve time."

"Legally, the mad can't be punished. But doesn't guilt often drive criminals mad? And doesn't madness drive people to commit heinous crimes?"

"I was told that the Ikuta Clinic doesn't admit such people."

"Perhaps madness is itself wrong, from humanity's perspective, even if you don't commit a crime of the sort you can see, a crime that hurts another person, or society."

"If so, I guess every human wrong deserves our pity. After all, each of us carries inside of us the potential for madness, don't you think?"

"I think what I heard in the tolling of the bell was deeper than that, or if not deeper at least less easily understood," Kuno said. "At any rate, don't many of the techniques doctors use in asylums resemble the efforts of the chaplain, or the confessor?"

"I'm sure they do. But as you said, that's a different issue."

"Ah."

"And this noble confessor—where would we find him?"

"For starters, I'd say there's one inside each of us."

"I see. And you would say the one inside you is *noble*?"

"Certainly," Kuno replied right away; then, needled by this answer, he paused. "If the part of me that forces me to answer for myself isn't noble, then the whole thing becomes silly and vulgar. More ludicrous, even, than feeling regret."

"I understand." Ineko's mother nodded. Then, "So did it sound to you as if you were the one striking the bell?"

"If they had let me strike it, I might have hit it so hard it would have cracked, more wildly than someone who was already mad—as if striking the bell were actually driving me insane. If we're all struggling to contain the madness inside us, what's wrong with losing our sanity for a while as we ring a bell?"

"Temple bells aren't formed that way. Not like these Western instruments everyone is so crazy about these days. I don't think Japan has ever had instruments like that—even those drums they beat so furiously at festivals. Aren't temple bells, up in the mountains, supposed to soothe the spirit? Isn't that how they're made?"

"What do you mean? How are they made?"

"The famous opening lines of *Tales of the Heike* capture it very well, I think: 'The Jetavana Temple bells / ring the passing of all things.' Those log-like hammers they use to strike the bells can't be swung in a way that produces such a crazy sound."

Kuno couldn't argue with this, but he wouldn't agree, either. "That 'passing of all things' stuff ... I don't hear that at all."

"Anyway, the doctors at the clinic let patients ring the bell because they think it may help. That's what they said. At least the effect it has is more natural than, say, sedatives or tranquilizers. Temple bells aren't percussion instruments."

"The doctor also said some of his colleagues can tell how a patient is doing just from the tone of the bell," Kuno said, not yet entirely calm. "And then he said that when patients strike the bell, the ringing may speak for them, give voice to something deep in their hearts."

"He did say that, yes."

"And you replied that that seemed a very sad thing to say, and the doctor said not necessarily—though honestly, he didn't really seem to be listening. You remember?"

"I'll never forget it. Even after Ineko leaves the clinic, I suspect," she said. "It won't ever be the way it was when Ineko rang the bell as a child, at Miidera. From now on, for the rest of my life, I'm sure I'll recall those words whenever I hear a Japanese temple bell."

"That one just now, at six, was another voice, another patient's heart."

"It didn't strike me as the voice of a confessor, though," the mother said. "There aren't any confessors at the clinic. Even if the doctors at asylums sometimes question patients in that fashion, I see no connection between that and the bell. I heard nothing like a confession, no repentance, no regret, no agony. I don't know, maybe a temple bell just isn't the best way of communicating the heart of the person striking it. Maybe I don't love my daughter as deeply as you do, Mr. Kuno."

"Our love is different, that's all."

"That said, if it sounded to you like your own confessor striking the bell ... I can't really comment on that, of course, and neither can anyone else, but it does say something."

"Nothing in me made it sound that way," Kuno said emphatically. "It was a confessor striking the bell, that's all there is to it. A noble confessor."

"Perhaps you're a little mad yourself, Mr. Kuno? First you see a non-existent white rat on the riverbank, and now all this about the bell."

Kuno wasn't having any of it. "Not at all."

"There are no confessors at clinics," Ineko's mother said calmly. "Though I guess the way you describe it, many of the mad are like that, forcing themselves to answer for themselves—they're just much purer at heart, or much weaker, than other people."

"That's exactly what I was saying."

"That it was one of the crazies?"

"Yes."

"But you can't say which of them was striking the bell. Just from the sound."

"I can, actually."

Ineko's mother widened her eyes. "Who?"

"It was him."

"Him?"

"The old man. I'm sure of it."

"What old man?"

"Bald, missing teeth, so thin he was like a sack of bones. You saw him—practicing his calligraphy."

"Ah, him? *To enter the Buddha world is easy; to enter the world of demons is difficult.* That's what he was writing. It stuck in my mind, because I remember seeing it on a scroll by Ikkyū," said Ineko's mother, keeping her gaze trained on Kuno's face. "You think an old wreck like him would have the strength to strike the bell? He could hardly stand."

"I do."

"And it would sound like a confessor?" she asked incredulously. "Doesn't that seem a bit delusional?"

"It's not a delusion. It's an instinct, a sixth sense," Kuno said. "Old Nishiyama may have been a wreck, falling apart at the seams, but did you notice his eyes? Did you see his face, how he held himself?"

"No. I didn't really look."

"The moment I saw him, I sensed that he had committed some terrible crime. Murder, maybe, or worse. They could have put him in jail or sentenced him to death, but instead they committed him. Perhaps the statute of limitations had expired."

"You think?" Ineko's mother, startled, mulled this over. "Why would you want to look at things this way? How awful."

"Awful—me?" Kuno shook his head. "If anyone is awful, it's him."

"Are you suggesting, Mr. Kuno, that he feigned madness while he waited for the statute of limitations to run out?"

"I have no idea. If he did, then obviously he managed to deceive the detectives and the police and so on, so I'd certainly never know. I have no relationship to him—I've only seen him once. Maybe he lost his mind after he committed the crime ... or before."

"You seem convinced that he's a criminal. Why?"

"You really didn't notice his eyes? The doctor said he sometimes loses his temper when he does his calligraphy, that he has spasms. Who knows what's happening then? If you ask me, the trembling is probably brought on by remorse, or horror. The old man's eyes were pools of criminality, the worst you can imagine. Of course, his pupils had a white cast—the doctor said he has cataracts. And what does that phrase mean, anyway? 'To enter the Buddha world is easy; to enter the world of demons is difficult.' I bet every so often he snaps out of it, and being in his true, sane state terrifies him so much that he has one of his fits."

"You've only seen him once, as you said," Ineko's mother said softly. "You don't think you're reading too much into things?"

"Perhaps, Mother, perhaps," Kuno replied. "But even that emaciated body of his looked to me like the embodiment of some old crime, grown withered and wrinkled."

"Really? I wonder."

"That phrase, 'To enter the Buddha world ...'—it's a zen thing?"

"I believe so. I'm not sure, but I think I saw it at a tea ceremony, on the scroll in the alcove. It was Ikkyū's calligraphy."

"I doubt the old man is seeking some profound zen insight with that phrase, in writing it again and again, day after day. He probably doesn't even see it as a meaningful paradox. He's using the second half to dull his guilt, that's all. Or more shamelessly still, to affirm his crime."

"A rite of atonement, you mean. His calligraphy."

"I guess, putting it in the most positive light, you could see it that way."

"It doesn't seem like something anyone truly mad would do."

"No, I doubt he's completely mad," Kuno said. "Except that ... well, it does seem crazy to go on writing the same phrase over and over."

"Supposing he really did commit some heinous crime," the mother said, her tone no less calm than before. "You think that would make his bell-ringing sound as if a confessor were doing it? And not just a confessor, but a *noble* confessor?"

"Obsessed with evil, or noble. One or the other."

"Still I doubt he's strong enough to strike such a large bell, and produce that sound."

"Maybe when he strikes the bell a weird kind of energy, a demonic force, wells up in him. There's probably a sort of rhythm to it, too—how you swing the hammer. You get used to it, in other words. I assume they let him do it all the time."

"I still don't see how you can be so sure it was him just now, at six."

"What have I been saying all long? It sounded like an inquisition."

"And I keep saying the same thing back. You're hearing something in your own heart."

"It's true, there may be something wrong with me." Kuno said bluntly. "But my certainty that it was him striking the bell has nothing to do with that."

Ineko's mother stared at Kuno for a moment, then looked down. "Mr. Kuno, we seem to have been going in circles all this time. Why is that, do you think?"

"Have we been going in circles?" Kuno asked. Then, as if to himself, "The next time they ring the bell is at nine. Maybe I should go up to the clinic and ring it myself."

"What?" The mother raised her eyes.

"I wonder how it would sound to you, if I did," Kuno said quietly.

"The doctors would never let you, Mr. Kuno. Even if they did, striking a hanging bell isn't like playing a regular instrument from sheet music. Those giant posts they use aren't made in such a way that you could bang the bell like crazy, as you said—so hard the metal cracks."

"I was thinking of ringing it with Ineko, actually," Kuno said quietly, almost sadly.

The mother seemed shocked. "With Ineko? I doubt they would permit that, either. Ineko struck the bell at three, to see us off. Besides, they're unlikely to admit visitors at night."

"They may have a rule against that, it's true. But there are exceptions. Even at an asylum, they must make allowances for extraordinary circumstances."

"Extraordinary circumstances? What do you mean?"

"No matter how many times I try, I can't convince you that it was the old man just now, ringing the six o'clock bell." Kuno had grown agitated again. "Couldn't you hear the difference, Mother? Between the bell Ineko rang at three, and the one at six—the old man's?"

"No, honestly, I couldn't. It was weak and unsteady when Ineko was striking it; I suppose whoever did it at six sounded more practiced."

"That's all? I guess as you age, little by little, the doors to your sensations close. Perhaps your eardrums grow less sensitive."

"That could be. But you hear the bell's ringing through your feelings. You admitted there's something wrong with you."

"There will be if I don't do something." Kuno paused. "We just left Ineko at an asylum. You understand that, don't you?"

"To cure her." The mother's tone, too, grew sharper. "I said earlier that maybe I don't love my daughter as deeply as you do, Mr. Kuno. That's quite a thing to say. But a mother loves her child as only a mother can. And all the sorrow we have endured over the years, since her father's death—the two of us, on our own, mother and daughter . . . ."

"I know, I understand. Are you suggesting I'm trying to steal her from you?"

"Pardon me? When have I ever interfered with your relationship?"

"Perhaps I tried to remove the part of you that's inside Ineko."

"Oh, that's okay. There's no escaping that anyway, no preventing it. I'll be fine as long as you two are happy, even if I end up all alone in an old-folks home or some such place."

"That's not what I'm saying. But don't you think you may have doted on her too much, when it was just the two of you? Handled her too carefully, as if you were cradling a precious jewel in your palm?"

"A jewel? That may be true." A sad look came over Ineko's mother's face. "But remember, Mr. Kuno, that she saw her father fall to his death from a cliff when she was just a girl, right in front of her. I'm her mother. I may have tried too hard to heal that wound, and been more solicitous than is normal."

"Well, *this* certainly isn't normal. Why put her in a madhouse?"

"To cure her, that's the only reason."

"Even after I said I would marry her, and cure her myself. Even when I tried to stop you. When you saw the trunk of that tree at clinic, all scratched up, you said it looked like it was crying . . . How can you be so oblivious to the tears streaming deep in our two hearts, lovers separated, one in the clinic, one outside?"

"Ineko has somagnosia. I thought marrying you would make it worse."

"May I ask when her somagnosia first appeared?"

"Hmm. I'm not entirely sure myself. Ineko says she screamed and covered her eyes when her father's horse went off the cliff, and then fainted, right there on her horse's back. She was still sitting there when they found her. And yet she also claims to have witnessed her father's death, the entire thing. She believes that. I don't know if she saw it with her actual eyes, or with the eyes of her conscience, but she's sure she saw it. My own sense is that there's no way a girl as young as she was then could have taken it all in so precisely, so objectively. I think she must have covered her eyes with her hands, and didn't really see anything. It's not like a car crash—it would have taken some time for him to fall from the top of the cliff all the way down to the water. I've never doubted her story, though. She may have had her hands over her actual, physical eyes, but seen it all with the eyes of her heart. I've always accepted what she says as the truth, and I've never questioned her in a way that might suggest that I'm skeptical. Not once. But you know, Mr. Kuno, it does seem a trifle odd to me that a man should sink immediately from view while the horse floats on the waves, kicking desperately. I mean, even supposing the man was dead already, and only the horse was still breathing."

"Maybe Father hit the water in the wrong way," Kuno said hesitantly. He'd never seen a man sink, or a horse kicking among the waves, so he had no idea what to say. It struck him, too, that Ineko's mother seemed somewhat out of sorts as she spoke, that there was something a little odd in her manner.

"Perhaps horses are more solidly built than people?"

"That's possible."

"Kizaki was an excellent swimmer. I remember hearing that he once won a long-distance swim race in Chiba, before he enlisted."

"Ah." Kuno glanced at the mother. Ineko's father had lost a leg. Even if he could still swim, he must have been dead by the time he hit the water. Kuno wasn't quite sure what the mother was trying to say. Perhaps he had left her feeling similarly unsettled when he let it slip that he found her handling of Ineko, once it was just the two of them, abnormally careful.

"You said you think Ineko saw her father's fall, the whole thing, in great detail, with the eyes of her conscience, the eyes of her heart, something like that ... so in your view, is that what her somagnosia is all about?" Kuno asked.

"No, it's not that." The mother shook her head. "After all, that's not a form of blindness. She saw everything then, whether it was through her conscience or her heart. Even if you're not seeing something with your actual eyes, you still see it. It's not blindness."

"Okay. You could say the same of dreams, too," Kuno said. "Maybe she did see it all, then. You forget your dreams once you wake, of course, but as long as you're dreaming, you see what you see. Which would you say has a more solid existence—something that catches your eye in a random dream, or something that is real but invisible?"

"Mr. Kuno," the mother said. "Ineko stops seeing things that are right there in front of her. We're not talking about a random dream."

"No, because in the real world you can reach out and touch a thing to confirm its existence, even if you can't see it."

"And doesn't that make it even scarier?" Ineko's mother caught her breath; her face grew somewhat red. "Mr. Kuno, it's awkward for me to talk about things like this, but supposing you were lying with Ineko, and she could touch you with her hands but not see you. Don't you think that would be terrifying—enough to drive a person mad?"

"Ah."

"How did you love Ineko, Mr. Kuno?"

"How did I love her?" Mr. Kuno mumbled, blushing in spite of himself. "How did I love her ... the truth is, there's no good way to answer that question. A man can love a woman in countless ways, it seems, but since I've only ever loved Ineko, I've never had an opportunity to compare techniques—to think about how it was with someone then, and how it is now with her."

"Thank you for that." The mother lowered her head. "Forgive me for asking."

"I think it was the same for Ineko. I don't believe she succumbed to somagnosia because I loved her differently from some man she knew before me. I doubt she stopped seeing me so that she could picture another man while I loved her."

"Of course not," said the mother hurriedly. "You can rest assured of that. Have faith in her, please. You knew that without my saying it, I'm sure, just from how she was with you."

"Yes."

"It's odd for me to be telling you this, Mr. Kuno, but it was the same for me—Ineko's father was the only man I ever knew. Before the war, there was a time when dancing was all the rage, and I did sometimes dance with other officers, holding their hands, and maybe I'd go out for a meal with one of them, but that's not really anything, is it?" said the mother. "I shouldn't have asked you that, about how you loved her. I'm sorry."

"That's all right. I'm sure it's only natural to wonder, as her mother."

"It's crazy—especially for someone with as little experience in love as I have—to be asking about another woman, another man—how they loved. I know that."

"I've read about all sorts of different styles and states of mind, in books and magazines and so on. But knowing something intellectually and actually experiencing it, so that it touches you in a deeper way—those are two entirely different things. Reading a work of fiction, I can't reach out with this hand of mine and actually touch a lover depicted there." Kuno realized he had let himself go. Abashed, he lowered his voice. "As I said, I have no idea if my loving of her was utterly ordinary, just like what other men do, or abnormally passionate. I'm young, and so of course my eye has occasionally been drawn to something in another young woman. But that's all. The way Ineko burrowed into my chest was different. And that was true of her, too—I never got the feeling she didn't like how I loved her, whether it was normal or not. I suppose it would have been awkward for you to ask her about such things."

Kuno realized, as he finished speaking, that Ineko's mother would interpret this as a clear admission that he had already slept with Ineko. There was no helping that.

Perhaps she had known all along, though, because she wasn't at all flustered.

"As far as I'm concerned, having Ineko stop seeing you while you held her wouldn't have been all that bad in itself. Personally, I'd find that terrifying, but … well, there's no actual danger in it, is there? But what if this was an early symptom of the onset of madness? What then? What if she succumbed to a somagnosic episode while she was out of the house? Then she'd really be in danger."

"I don't think her somagnosia would emerge in any other situation, only with people she loves, or is at least attracted to. My sense is that, if she were walking down the street and someone came along who meant nothing to her, nothing would ever happen."

"Even so, Mr. Kuno, say she was on a busy street, and she saw you on the other side and darted out into the road without seeing the cars zooming past, seeing only you—what would happen then? What if she were up on the roof of a train station or department store and she looked down the stairs and saw you, and jumped. What then?"

"Those examples are irrelevant. When she has an episode, the person she loves vanishes—no one else. So she'd see all the cars on the road, but not me on the other sidewalk. She wouldn't see me at the bottom of the stairs."

"Please don't make things up, Mr. Kuno," the mother said sternly. "Would you have me believe she never saw you at all? That she loved you without ever seeing you?"

"Certainly not."

"Of course not. That's impossible. She just stopped seeing parts of you, at certain times and under certain circumstances."

"Ah."

"And that's a sign of madness, and madness progresses, and there's no way of knowing how bad it may get."

"No, but it wasn't so bad that she had to be committed. I've told you over and over that I thought I could heal her if we got married." Kuno lowered his voice. "You believe you can cure her by taking her away from me for a while, perhaps a long while. Isn't that right? Even if it means abandoning your young, lovely daughter in a crowd of rough, dirty madmen."

A look of terrible loneliness flickered into Ineko's mother's eyes. "You know, Mr. Kuno," she said, not quite crying. "You know all I want is to cure her madness before the marriage. It's only natural, isn't it, for a mother to feel that way? Please understand. I searched all over for the right clinic, you know that. You mustn't call it a mad-house … that's not true, it's a clinic with a psychiatric ward, a neuro-logical ward. That's what it is."

"I know. The Ikuta Clinic, here in Ikuta. It's like a dandelion, it has all the warmth of a field—I acknowledge that. They even let the patients strike the temple bell."

"Exactly."

"But, Mother, which do you think can cure Ineko? The Ikuta Clinic, or me?"

"I was afraid her condition might worsen. That's all."

"You think she's really mad, mother?"

"I'm her mother. Others may think she is, but I won't ever believe it—I couldn't."

"Her optic nerve blinks out from time to time, that's all. Not even the whole thing, just a bit. At least, that's all I ever saw. Is that mad-ness?" Kuno's breath had quickened. "It makes no sense to me, it really doesn't, that she agreed to go stay in that clinic, all alone."

"It's because I pleaded with her, Mr. Kuno," Ineko's mother said sadly. "Because I told her that if she loved you, if she wanted to marry you, she had to get better first. I kept at it until she consented."

"Ineko isn't crazy, it's just a little nervous trouble. Or did she ex-hibit other symptoms at home with you, when I wasn't around? Did she rave like a lunatic? I doubt she showed any signs of this sex mania you hear about—people throwing off their clothes and running out naked into the street."

"Of course not. However depressed she got, the most she did was sit and stare blankly into space. She was probably with you then, too, in her heart. She never behaved in a manner that was in any way untoward. To be honest, I agonized over the decision, I truly did, wondering whether she mightn't get better if you married her right away. But when I talked to the neurologist, he said it could be quite scary—this rare disease, somagnosia."

"It isn't. Not at all."

"The doctor once told me about a woman who had it. I'm sure I told you the story. She was a young woman, a brand new mother, and she ended up strangling her baby because she couldn't see its head. She could feel it, but . . . ."

"Ineko is too weak to do something like that—she could squeeze my neck as hard as she liked and she still couldn't kill me. I've told you that before, too, I know. Besides, even if she did somehow manage to kill me, I can't think of anything that would make me happier."

"People talk of the strength of madmen."

"Ineko isn't mad. Sanity and madness are two sides of the same coin. And that's true of ordinary people and of geniuses—geniuses have the same uncontrollable strength you're talking about. Sometimes they're abnormally powerful, sometimes abnormally weak. Sometimes it's mental, sometimes physical. The fingers of a master shakuhachi player and a skilled masseur will both be equally deformed, equally bent out of shape. That's not a very pleasant example, I know."

"Ineko isn't a master of anything. Just an ordinary young woman."

"Most people think of themselves as ordinary. And yet somewhere deep in their hearts, they take pride in being different from other people, better than them. They won't usually tell you that's how they feel, but I'm sure they do. Surely you know that even better than I do, Mother, seeing as you've lived so many more years than I have. You must have seen people behave that way before the war—the officers you knew must have had some strengths of their own, after all."

"Individualism, they call it. Obviously, no two people are the same."

"Not even the wicked ones. We call people villains or madmen if they disrupt our societies, but history offers countless examples of people like that who have come to be venerated in later ages."

"Yes, I know," the mother murmured. "But it's true, Mr. Kuno, Ineko is a very ordinary young woman. I suspect you'd be disappointed if you married her. *So this is what she's really like!* you'd think. Perhaps as a parent I shouldn't say this, but whatever attractions she may have for you now won't mean a thing once you're married. Those sensuous, dark eyes, and long, thick eyelashes, for instance. The lovely, clean curves of her legs . . . ."

"And her somagnosia won't mean anything, either, will it?"

"You're right that it's an uncommon defect of the nerves, an abnormality. But, as you so graciously suggested, maybe not a form of madness."

"It's not as if she can't see me at all, you know."

"Yes." Ineko's mother regarded Kuno. "But Mr. Kuno, I'm told it's not entirely unheard of for somagnosia of the nerves to worsen over time." She paused. "That was the case with the woman who throttled her baby. Have you ever seen that Goya painting of the man eating his child, beginning with the head? The father tugging so hard that the bloody neck has become elongated? Not that I'm comparing Ineko to a genius like Goya."

"I've seen it. I'm sure if Goya had been a somagnosiac, he would have created even more eerie images of headless bodies, and people with no torsos." Despite the grim topic, a faint smile played across his lips. "At any rate, Ineko's somagnosia couldn't be more different from Goya's late works—her condition is rooted in love. A woman's love, almost excessively pure. I truly believe that. And I know I'm not wrong."

A woman came in to take away the dishes from dinner. She was different from the one who'd come before. Her shoulders sloped down in a manner one didn't often see among young women these days. Her body seemed unnaturally narrow from the chest up.

She eyed the grilled fish Ineko's mother had left untouched, and the mostly uneaten sashimi.

"What time would you like me to prepare the futons?" she asked.

"Nine or ten, maybe?" Ineko's mother said at first. Then, "Actually, any time is fine. We don't have anything to do other than go to bed."

"As you wish."

"How about a bath?" Kuno looked at Ineko's mother.

"I'd be happy to draw one if you would like," said the woman.

"There's no need if no one else is going to use it. Are we the only guests?" Ineko's mother asked the woman, then turned to Kuno. "Is that all right, Mr. Kuno?"

"Yes, I'm fine." Kuno nodded. "I don't need a bath. This town is, how should I put it—I feel as if its lovely, gentle mood is seeping into my skin. I wouldn't want to wash it off."

"I'll prepare the bath right away," the woman said, and left.

Ineko's mother eyed the shabby, aging ceiling, and the sliding doors. "I wonder what the bath is like. Going in alone might be a bit creepy. Just thinking about it makes my skin crawl, right around here." She touched the nape of her neck with her left hand. "Why don't you go first, Mr. Kuno? See what it's like."

"I wonder ..." Kuno seemed to have been struck by a thought. "What sort of bath do you think they have at the clinic?"

"At the clinic?"

"Even madhouses must have baths, right? Even madmen bathe. Do you think they have a big bath, and Ineko goes in with all those crazy people?"

"I'm not sure if they bathe together. That's a good question."

"That would be dreadful. Just thinking about it makes me shudder."

Both Ineko's mother and Kuno were calling up an image of Ineko's lovely, naked body. Naturally, Kuno could picture her more clearly.

"Think of that woman with the matted hair, and the one with the slanted eyes, and Ineko right there in the water with them. There was another as gaunt as a hungry ghost. I wouldn't be surprised if she gets dirt caught in the valleys between her ribs. Some of them won't have had their nails cut. Their skin looked odd, too, no? Maybe certain tones are characteristic of the mad? Some had a deathly look, with swarthy skin; others were so white it made you feel weird just looking at them."

"Hmm."

"When Ineko gets in there among the rest of them with her gorgeous skin ... they might become so agitated that they scratch her, tear her skin with their nails."

"Don't say such things." Ineko's mother cut him off. "I'm sure that won't happen, and I don't want to picture it."

"We left Ineko at the clinic, so we have no choice but to think of her there. That's just as true for you as it is for me."

Tonight, in this tranquil town, even the ocean made no sound. You knew it was out there, yet you couldn't hear it. The silence seemed to call up a memory in Ineko's mother. It was a memory of Ineko, of course. After Kuno went off to the bath, leaving her alone, she kept thinking about it. Then he came back.

"How was it?" she asked him.

"Not very nice. Dim, chilly. You might be better off skipping the bath."

"You think? Maybe, even so ..." Ineko's mother got to her feet without looking at him. She couldn't tell Kuno about that particular memory of Ineko.

"It's full of steam, so I doubt it will be cold anymore," Kuno said to her back.

The bath was small for an inn, and so ancient you could see a buildup of grime between the boards, yet when Ineko's mother crouched down and splashed hot water around her waist with a bucket, she felt her body unclench. Once she was in the water, though, submerged to her shoulders, she was suddenly seized by a feeling of loneliness. Her eyes smarted.

After the loneliness faded, she grew uneasy. One of the windows faced the hall, while the other seemed to look out on the kitchen or something. The glass in both windows was frosted, but she was still unsettled by unlikely possibilities—someone might be peering in at her, or open one of the windows. Or then again, that Kuno might take advantage of her absence to slip out of the inn and go visit Ineko at the clinic, or bring her back out. Ineko's mother hurried back to the room.

"It was kind of unpleasant, wasn't it?" Kuno said when he saw her.

"I suppose."

"Maybe it's only to be expected at a place like this."

"That's probably true."

Ineko's mother sat down at the plain dresser in the next room. There was no cushion on the floor in front of it. Even though she had just come from the bath, she didn't do much to her face—a little lipstick, and that was it.

"I'd completely forgotten this, and it only came back to me as I was soaking in the water, but Ineko and I actually had a bath today, before we left the house. We thought it would feel good to get nice and clean beforehand. I washed her back for her. I wonder how long it's been since I did that. It's bizarre—I don't know how it could have slipped my mind. You and I were talking about the bath all that time, and it never once occurred to me. There must be something wrong with me, don't you think?" The whole time she was saying this, with a smile on her lips, she was sensing the touch of Ineko's skin. She even began to feel in her hands the smoothness of Ineko's skin when she was a baby, still breastfeeding.

Hearing that Ineko's mother had washed Ineko's body that morning, Kuno, too, started to remember the sensation of her skin on his. Naturally, he and Ineko's mother had gotten to know Ineko's skin in different ways. Their expressions gave no sign that they were busy savoring the touch of Ineko's skin, so neither suspected that this is what the other was thinking of.

"Maybe Ineko won't bathe at the clinic today, since you took a bath at home," Kuno said, rather oddly, hiding from the mother the vivid presence of Ineko's skin.

"Perhaps you're right," Ineko's mother replied absently.

She'd said she could hardly recall when she had last bathed with Ineko and washed her back, but how many years had it been? Truth be told, thinking in terms of years was already an exaggeration — most likely, it had been a matter of months, maybe days. She bathed with her daughter all the time, so she never gave it any thought. Only today she had. That was what had prompted her to use those words. *How many years?*

The mother had rested her left hand on Ineko's shoulder, and then with her right she washed her daughter's back. Doing so made her sad. As she lifted up her daughter's hair and scrubbed the nape of her neck, some of the shorter hairs at the back picked up a bit of lather. Ineko's mother felt the desire to wash her daughter's hair.

"You've got a lot of these short hairs," the mother said, touching them with her hand.

"I do." Ineko nodded. "You can tell when I tie up my hair in the back."

"When was the last time you washed your hair?"

"Let's see ... four days ago. Didn't I tell you? When I went to the beauty parlor."

"That's right, I remember."

"Does it smell?"

The mother leaned so close that her nose brushed Ineko's hair. She felt the urge to wrap her arms around her daughter. "No, doesn't."

"That tickles." The mother's hand was nearly under Ineko's arm. She sat up and poured another bucket of hot water over her daughter's back.

Ineko's mother cast her thoughts back to the time when she and her daughter had always bathed together, as if they had reached some tacit agreement that they should. She remembered how worried she had been about Ineko's right nipple, which when she was a girl had been flat, or even concave. Her mother's gaze had had a tendency to linger there, on that right nipple that was so different from the left. Then at some point the right nipple had become fuller. It was still slightly smaller than the left, but the difference was so insignificant that you couldn't see it unless you were looking. What had made that one nipple grow more slowly than the other? Ineko's mother didn't really think there was any link between the nipple and Ineko's bouts of madness, yet it troubled her in a way no other part of her daughter's body did. Her daughter's body was beautiful. She loved it that her toes were so short and her fingers so long.

One day, Ineko had seemed hesitant to bathe together. Her mother guessed it was because Ineko had slept with Kuno. Or perhaps her suspicion that they had slept together was what made her think Ineko was hesitant. Maybe Ineko hadn't been acting any different from usual, and her mother had simply been watching too closely. By then, they were no longer in the habit of bathing together every time they bathed. There had been no clear break, no special day after which they stopped bathing together as much; it had happened as a matter of course as Ineko grew older. But that was the first time Ineko had ever seemed to hesitate.

She assumed her daughter didn't want to be seen after having been with a man for the first time, that it was as simple as that. That seemed natural enough, not unexpected, and yet at the same time surprising. She tried to recall her own first night. She suspected nothing, of course, of the fear and distress that had seized Ineko when she stopped seeing the man in her arms.*

---

* Please see the translator's afterword (p. 121) regarding some temporal inconsistencies in the pages that follow.

Once when she was in eleventh grade, Ineko had come to her mother, pale and shaking, and told her about how, during a ping-pong game, in the middle of a volley, she had suddenly lost sight of the ball. Ineko was an alternate on the school ping-pong team. The day before, Ineko had mentioned that she had a class tournament the next day. It was a Saturday, and Ineko's mother had assumed she would return home somewhat late, but she didn't, and a friend had walked her all the way home.

Ineko's mother heard her friend calling, and went to the door.

"Ineko—what's wrong?" the mother cried.

"She suddenly started feeling ill, so our teacher asked us to take her home." The friend put her arm around Ineko's back as she spoke, as if to support her, and peered at her face.

Ineko stepped away, avoiding her friend's touch. She couldn't see her friend's face, or her mother's. She was about to step up from the entryway into the house when she reached out her right hand and lightly squeezed her friend's palm. Evidently she meant this as an expression of gratitude. She didn't smile, though, or look back; she just walked straight down the hall and disappeared into the house. Ineko was so gentle and polite that it was almost inconceivable that she should behave this way. The friend, whose name was Yōko, came over all the time and treated Ineko as an older sister, so maybe it wasn't necessary for Ineko to thank her for anything—but more than that was going on here. Ineko's mother could tell from the movement of her daughter's feet as she walked away that she wasn't feeling all that unwell, so she almost smiled as she apologized.

"I'm sorry, Yōko. What can have gotten into her?"

Yōko stared blankly after Ineko. "Please go see how she is doing. She seems a bit strange. I won't stay."

Then, speaking rapidly, she had explained what had happened. Twice during a game Ineko had returned the ball in a very odd way, snapping her hand at the wrist like an automaton, and then the third time she had missed the ball all together—or rather simply stood dazed for a moment before suddenly putting her hands over her eyes and collapsing right there in front of the table. She had knelt down on the floor, slumped forward.

The girl she had been playing with just stared. She said later that she thought Ineko must have gotten dizzy or had an anemic spell, but in the heat of the game it was all she could do to stop and stand still. Yōko had been the one to run to Ineko's side.

"I'm fine," Ineko said. Yōko stroked Ineko's hair. Then, perhaps realizing that this was a bit odd under the circumstances, she put her right arm around Ineko's shoulder and touched her forehead with her left hand. Ineko's forehead wasn't cool to the touch; if anything, it felt warm. The dampness Yōko felt wasn't a cold sweat; it was just sweat from exertion.

"You're okay, then?" Yōko had said. "Thank goodness."

Ineko stood up, slipping free of Yōko's arm. "I'm fine."

Then, as if it were the most natural thing in the world that she should do so, she stepped away from the ping-pong table. The question of whether or not she ought to go on with the game seemed never even to have crossed her mind. She kept her head down, saying nothing, and though she was still pale, she didn't look so weak that she would need to be escorted home. When Yōko kept hovering about, having been directed to do so by their teacher, Ineko told her once again, "I'm okay, really. I'll go home alone. I'd rather go by myself." Then, "I'd like to be alone as soon as I can. Please, just leave me."

"I can't, the teacher asked me to stay."

"I just want to be left alone," Ineko mumbled. "I want to cry."

"To cry? You want to cry, is that what you said? How delightful," Yōko twittered merrily. "What fun that would be—you crying, me comforting you. What a miracle that would be!"

"You're exaggerating."

"You always see me crying. Every once in a while you should take a turn."

"I cry all the time, just not in public—not since my father died."

Yōko assumed Ineko was feeling down because she had lost her game. When they arrived at Ineko's house and Ineko abruptly ran off down the hall, she figured it was because she felt the need to be alone with her tears.

Ineko didn't turn to look when her mother opened her door. Even as her mother walked over, Ineko's gaze remained fixed on her left hand where it lay on her desk, a pair of ping-pong balls cradled in her palm. She kept a few balls in her desk drawer, so their presence wasn't unexpected, but it felt odd to see her staring down at them so intently, as if she didn't know what they were. Not surprisingly, her mother came to the same conclusion as Yōko—Ineko was just feeling annoyed with herself for having lost the game.

"How are you feeling? Shouldn't you be in bed, rather than sitting here?" the mother said, placing her hand on the back of Ineko's chair. "You didn't see the doctor at school, did you? Did you get any medicine?"

"No."

"But you saw the doctor?"

"It's nothing."

"We don't need to call him?"

"No."

"What's gotten into you, taking out those balls? Put them back. It makes you seem like a sore loser. It wasn't your fault—don't dwell on it. Here, put them away." The mother lifted the balls from Ineko's hand. "Take it easy in bed until dinner. You look pale. Would you like some coffee, or maybe some tea?"

"I don't feel like it." Ineko held out her hand. "Give them back."

"These?"

Ineko's mother watched as her daughter placed the balls back on her palm, stared at them for a moment, and then returned them to the drawer.

As she looked up, Ineko's eyes were drawn to the redness of the blooms on the camellia trees in the garden. The flowers were startlingly numerous. There were four or five trees, all quite old, their branches wide, taller than is typical for their kind. The presence of so many blossoms lent a certain airiness, a brightness, to the otherwise massy appearance of the deep green leaves. The roof's shadow extended halfway up the trees, marking the arrival of winter.

"They've bloomed nicely," Ineko's mother said.

"They're just getting started. Look at all those buds," Ineko said. "Early in the season Father used to come in constantly to see if they had started opening."

"He came in all the time, not just in camellia season."

"But especially then. Camellia season just happens to be extremely long." For the first time since she had come home, Ineko smiled.

"They bloom right up until spring, until it's time for the cherries," Ineko's mother replied. "Did you hurt yourself during the game, Ineko? You haven't told me anything. Did the ball hit you?"

"I couldn't see it."

"You couldn't see the ball?"

"No. It disappeared."

"What do you mean, it disappeared? The other girl hit it too fast? You got dizzy?"

"No, everything was perfectly ordinary. And then suddenly I couldn't see the ball."

"Why not?"

"I have no idea."

"Did you feel ill?"

"Oh, if only I had. But it wasn't that—I didn't feel lightheaded. I was standing up straight, and I could see everything else, only the ball was gone."

"How can that be?" Ineko's mother asked skeptically. "I don't see how you could have been paying attention to anything else. When you're in the midst of a game, don't you have to focus so completely on the ball that you stop seeing anything else? That sort of blindness is just part of the game."

"That's not what I'm saying," Ineko replied forcefully. "It was the ball that was gone."

"You must be mistaken. Your recalling it that way proves you weren't feeling well."

Ineko seemed not even to have heard her mother's words. Still gazing out at the garden—her eyes turned toward the camellias, that is to say, though she wasn't looking at them—she said in a subdued tone, "Even so, Mother, even without seeing the ball, I managed to return it twice, I think. I guess I could tell where the ball was going from how the other girl's body moved, her arms, and I'm experienced enough that my hand went to the right place on its own. Realizing that made me twice as scared, maybe even three times. Being unable to see the ball, and hitting it anyway. My whole chest seized up, I was so frightened; I couldn't even move."

"Is that true?" Ineko's mother couldn't see how all that could be, and yet she couldn't very well question Ineko's story. She sensed something of Ineko's terror, and kept quiet.

After a moment, Ineko spoke again. "Mother, did you know blind people play ping-pong, too?" It was clear from her tone how fiercely she was struggling to remain calm.

"What?" The mother stared blankly at Ineko. "They can do that?"

"Yes, actually."

"I know the blind have good instincts. But ping-pong?"

"They put little grains of lead in the balls so they rattle when they move. They track the movements by the sound."

"Really? That's amazing."

"The tables are sloped. They're higher in the middle, and lower on either side. They have a rim around the edge, too, to keep the ball from rolling off. There's a net, but it's not like a regular net—it's open underneath. You hit the ball under the net, in other words. If the ball goes too high, it hits the net."

"The ball goes under the net?"

"That's right."

"So essentially you're rolling the ball?"

"They do the same thing in blind baseball. Hit the ball so it rolls."

Ineko had watched blind students play ping-pong and baseball at a school for the blind. She continued talking for a while about that experience.

Her mother focused more on Ineko's tone and expression than on what she was saying. She wondered, hearing about the kids playing baseball, whether they could still roll the balls, or track the noises the balls made, if they were completely blind, because they had gotten used to playing that way and had honed their instincts, or if this was something only the partially blind or those who simply had poor vision did. She didn't ask. She had trouble gleaning from Ineko's explanation how the students would hit the ball or play defense, but she just went on listening, occasionally emitting a noncommittal murmur, a vague expression on her face that suggested neither comprehension nor confusion.

Ineko paused for a moment. "When did you visit the school and see those games?" her mother asked lightly.

"We went on a field trip in middle school."

"In middle school? I wonder if you told me about it then."

"I'm sure I must have. I think I did."

"Really?" The mother, who had been examining Ineko's face, lowered her eyes. "I'm not sure I ever heard about that before. I don't recall you telling me."

"I can't imagine that I wouldn't."

"That's true. You probably would have. Back then you used to run through everything that had happened during the day when you got back from school, in a big rush. You still do, I guess, though you don't talk so fast now. You used to launch into your stories the moment you got home, speaking ridiculously fast … and I loved that. It was like a bell calling my life back to me, after I had spent the whole day at home alone." Ineko's mother paused. "How strange. You really think you told me about that trip?"

"I'm sure I did. I told you, and you forgot."

"But that's crazy. You'd think I would remember hearing it. It's an unusual story, after all. And yet I have no recollection."

"That's odd." Ineko, too, looked worried. "Maybe I didn't tell you? I can't see why I wouldn't have, though, if I didn't. Why would I keep quiet about something like that?"

"You would have to answer that question, not me."

"You really don't think you've heard about this before?"

"I think this must be the first time."

"Really?" Ineko seemed somewhat suspicious of herself now, but that doubt seemed to be helping her regain her composure, little by little.

"When you told me about it just now …" the mother said. "Didn't it seem like you were telling me for the first time?"

Ineko was skeptical. "That's absurd. You can't judge from *how* I told you. It's a very unusual thing, Mother, blind ping-pong, and baseball, and it's not easy to picture it if you've never seen it. You have to make it novel if you're going to try and explain it."

"Novel?"

"Or singular. We just learned those words at school. Novel and singular. My friends and I use them a lot these days, to practice. 'Novel' came up just the other day."

"I see. Still, if you think about it, Ineko, when you started just now, with your 'novel' way of telling me about that trip, you asked if I knew that blind people play ping-pong. That was the very first thing you said. I don't think you would have begun with that question if you had already told me once before."

"Oh, *mom*," Ineko said, stretching out the syllables the way she used to when she wanted something from her mother as a little girl. This made her mother feel a little calmer. Ineko went on, as if she what she was saying were utterly obvious. "That's basic conversation. It's one of the easiest, most basic techniques. When you're telling someone something unusual, or when you want to draw someone in, you start out with a question like that, right?"

"But in this case—"

"What?"

"I still feel," Ineko's mother said, "as if this is the first time I've heard it." Her eyes clouded, as if she were combing through her memories, and finding nothing.

Ineko regarded her for a moment, then lowered her voice. "You think so? You honestly think I never told you about that?"

"I don't think I'd forget something like that. A story like that leaves an impression. Even if I didn't recall the details, I think I would at least remember having heard it."

"Yes." Ineko nodded. "But if I didn't tell you, why didn't I?"

"That I don't know." The mother smiled gently. "Anyway, that's enough. We don't need to get so hung up on whether or not you told me. Let's just let it go."

"It's a problem, though," Ineko said. "It could be. A little bit."

If anything, all this was more of an issue for Ineko's mother than for Ineko herself. To some extent, the mother had let this conversation continue for so long because she hoped it would give form to a certain vague unease that had been troubling her. Naturally, she tried hard not to reveal to Ineko, through either her tone or her expression, how she was feeling.

Unease wasn't even the right word—it was like the churning of a fog from which, at any moment, a feeling of unease might emerge. She had found herself wondering, all of a sudden, whether Ineko's becoming unable to see the ping-pong ball during her match that day might be connected in some obscure way to the fact that she had never mentioned that field trip, years ago, where she saw the blind students playing ping-pong and baseball. If there were some link, though, some connection, it would indeed be obscure—there was no other word for it—and she couldn't immediately recall any incident that might confirm its existence.

When Ineko herself referred to her silence about the trip as a problem, he tone had been casual. It didn't seem to have occurred to her, as it had to her mother, that there might be something darker there to explore. And yet she did return to it once more: "Why wouldn't I have told you, if it's true that I didn't? I can't figure it out. Maybe something happened that same day, something disturbing. Maybe I was too preoccupied with that to tell you about blind ping-pong. Maybe... but I don't remember anything happening."

Just then, Ineko's mother started thinking of something else. "You were so quick to cry when you were little," she said. "You used to feel sorry for the camellia blossoms when they dropped, so you would gather them up. Put them in envelopes, between the pages of a book. I never once saw you sweep the flowers up and throw them away."

"Not when I was little, no."

"You used to make cushions from flowers, too, stuffing them with dried camellia blossoms, winter daphne, violets. I remember you would embroider the covers, with a violet if a cushion was filled with violets, and so on. Even dried, the petals had a slight fragrance. They weren't particularly good as cushions, to tell the truth, but you put a lot of effort into them—each year, after a particular flower had bloomed, you would take out the old petals and replace them, or make a new cover and embroider it."

"Father liked those cushions. Their sweet smell."

"You even made one for his bed so he could enjoy the fragrance as he slept. It took a while for him to get used to it, and he wasn't sure he ever would."

"I remember."

"You once asked him, as serious as could be, how the trees in our garden ended up there. Couldn't they have bloomed somewhere else, you asked him, in the mountains or the woods, or in someone else's garden? You remember that, Ineko? At first he didn't know how to reply, but then after a moment he said that maybe the flowers wanted to be in his pillow, and that was why they came and blossomed here. That made sense to you. Yes, you told him, the trees and the flowers must be happy about that, too. And your father smiled and said you were the most adorable child, and he stroked your hair."

"He certainly did not stroke my hair. He grabbed one of my pigtails and yanked it two or three times in a row."

"I'm impressed you remember."

"Well, it hurt." Ineko looked out at the garden, at the camellias. She was thinking of her lover, Kuno, and how he liked to toy with her hair.

"That's the sort of girl you were," her mother said. Thinking not of Kuno, of course, but of Ineko gathering blossoms. "You felt sorry for fallen flowers."

"What made you think of that?" Inkeko asked.

"Actually," her mother replied without answering, "I remember your father said something else then, too, when you asked that childish, difficult question about why the trees in our garden grew there, and bloomed for us. He said trees have their own destiny."

"Did he?"

"Children ask difficult things, don't they?"

"They're amazed by everything," Ineko said. "When something impresses them, they start being struck by everything they see, each little event. Because they don't have any answers — why is it there, why did it happen? I think all children are that way. If a child finds a worm while she's digging in the garden and asks what it is, the adults will tell her it's a worm. There are worms in the soil? Why? That's just where they are, they live there, the adults tell her. This won't satisfy her, though. Because what amazes her isn't just that the worms live in the soil, it's the very fact of their existence — that the world is home to such creatures, so different from people that the two can't even be compared. That's what's beyond her, what dazzles her. When a mosquito bites her, she wants to know why. Because of course it ends up dead, right? She swats it with her hand and kills it. When I was small, I used to hate when it got dark at night, and so one day I asked Father why it couldn't always be daytime. And he said I wouldn't be able to sleep then, and neither would he. I remember that. So I asked him who made the night for us. That's a good question, he said. The god of sleep, I guess. There's a god of sleep? What kind of god is he? Where is he? Father gave the most absurd answers: you can't see him, he's asleep. Lies only a child would believe."

"Who made the night ... that's an interesting question," the mother replied.

"Of course nighttime doesn't exist to put humans to sleep; even if there were no people, the planet would still have nights. If anything, it's the opposite: we sleep because night exists."

"You think so? I doubt we would stop sleeping just because nighttime ceased to exist. Though this is all nonsense. Night does exist."

"And why is that? If I were still a child, I'm sure I'd ask. Children question things that are amazing to them, or that they can't comprehend, and then adults try to get out of answering with remarks about the difficult things children say."

"But truly difficult questions are just that, and there's no way to answer them. Night exists because it does; worms live in the soil because that's where they are. That's all there is to it—at least as far as ordinary people like us are concerned. Humans evolved on a planet that has nights, so it's in our nature to sleep at night. And the same goes for most animals."

"And ... ?"

"And what?"

"You were in the middle of saying something earlier. You were talking about what I was like as a child, how I used to feel sorry for flowers when their petals dropped, and I asked why you brought that up. That's how we got on this topic."

"Ah, that's right. I was just remembering your father's comment about how each tree has its own destiny, and that's what brought those trees to our garden." The mother's memory seemed to have been set in motion again. "You know he called you his little philosopher."

"I'd ask something difficult. He couldn't answer. And so he would try to put me off by calling me a philosopher—that's all it ever was. I remember saying that every child would be a little philosopher according to his definition, the younger, the more philosophical. Perhaps the origins of philosophy are there, in that period when infants start becoming aware of their surroundings, when they start to see, to remember words. And he said yes, that was probably true. That seemed like a good way to think about it. I remember the expression on his face as he nodded then, how he didn't seem to have given the slightest thought to what I had said. I mean, please … telling a little girl she's a philosopher? I even asked him what a philosopher was once, and he couldn't answer. A child wouldn't understand, he said. That was it."

"I couldn't explain philosophy myself, and I doubt you could, either. Although it's …." Her mother paused. "I suppose it involves feeling something, and then using that feeling as a starting point for a train of thought. The feeling itself may be naïve, a lingering sense of wonder at something most people take for granted but you hold on to it, and think it through as far as you can. Does that sound right?"

"Mother," Ineko said, her brow clouding suddenly. "When I stopped seeing the ball earlier, in the middle of the game, it wasn't because I took it for granted—and the experience wasn't exactly wonderful."

Even as the conversation moved back to the vanished ball, the mother struggled to hide her distress. "There has to be another explanation. It wasn't that you couldn't see it, you just thought you couldn't see it. For a moment. You returned the ball, didn't you? How could you hit a ball you can't see?"

"I do play ping-pong, Mother. My hand just knew where to go."

"I don't believe it. Tell me, did you feel that you had hit the ball?"

"That's a good point. I can't say for sure, but now that you've asked, I guess I'd say that I did feel I had." Ineko's eyelids trembled in a manner that suggested she was trying, but failing, to put herself back in the moment. "I'm really not sure. As you said, it was a reflexive motion, and it only lasted an instant."

"An instant so short you can't even say for sure that you didn't see the ball."

"No, I can. I know I didn't see it. When I realized I couldn't see it, I got so scared I just stood there, stunned, and then I bent down to the floor."

"You felt ill, that's all. You didn't faint, I know—maybe it was your nerves or something, maybe there's a bit that you're missing."

"Missing? My nerves?"

"Well, maybe not your nerves. Something. And I don't know if it's missing or you lost it or what. But isn't that how you felt? Vague, absent, dizzy?"

"No."

The mother gazed at Ineko for a moment without speaking. Then, lowering her voice, "It's possible to lose your memory, to have parts go missing. You know that, right? You remember what happened with your father?"

"Yes. That's my earliest memory."

"We weren't there, of course. We just heard about it from him."

"I believed it was all exactly as he said, that there really was a maiden or a sprite who served a god deep in the mountains, and she protected him, saved him. I was only three at the time. I was only three, and yet I still remember it, even now."

"The day Japan surrendered, your father was completely hollowed out, as they used to say—nowadays I guess you would say he was wiped out. In actuality, it was much worse than either phrase suggests. It wasn't just that a commanding officer had gone missing, and for a whole five days—for some significant portion of that time when he was wandering in the mountains, who knows how long, he had no awareness of himself. There was a period when he lost his memory, when bits of it vanished. It's even scarier than that, really, because he was on horseback. I'm almost positive that he stayed on his horse the whole time. Though he did get down in front of the camphor tree, that's clear."

"He rode back to his men, right? I remember hearing that."

"Yes, he rode back to his men," the mother said, repeating Ineko's words. "Though when you say his men ... it was headquarters, actually." She paused, then continued. "He would have had to get off his horse to carve his name on the trunk of that huge camphor. He said he had no recollection of who he was, even as he etched the characters with his sword. And no idea how he had come to be there, by that tree. No memory of it at all. And then a young woman from the mountains happened along and spoke to him, and he came to—that's what he said. She was so lovely and had such a noble air that she seemed like a heavenly maiden. That was how your father described her. A maiden in the service of a god, or maybe a sprite. They were so deep in the mountains that there wasn't even a path; the young woman couldn't possibly have gotten there on her own. Father had been carving his rank in the bark, Army Lieutenant Colonel, and when the woman saw the words she was startled, and she did all she could to nurse him, and that was how your father made it back down the mountain alive."

"Did he ever thank her? Did they exchange letters or anything?"

"Not as far as I know. I don't think they were ever in touch after he left."

"That's not nice. Assuming she was human."

"I doubt she was just an illusion. Though I'm sure at that moment he would have been grateful for anything that helped him survive, even a fantasy girl in the mountains. He had no idea what he was doing, it seems, but I think it's obvious that the words he was carving in the bark of that camphor tree must have been something like

Army Lieutenant Colonel Kizaki Masayuki ended his life on this spot.
He said when the young woman appeared, he had only made it as
far as *Army Lieutenant Colonel Ki . . . ."*

"He actually carved the characters? Even though he wasn't himself?"

"I wonder. I imagine they were at least legible."

"You've never seen them?"

"Of course not."

"Wouldn't you like to? I would. I'd want to very badly," Ineko said,
her voice growing more forceful. "I bet the writing is still there. It
must be."

"Probably. Until the tree dies, or gets chopped down. I've always
assumed the characters are still there on the trunk."

"Let's go find them, Mother. Will you take me there, please?"

"What a strange child you are, suddenly coming out with such a
thing. You realize it's in Kyūshū? Well, we can get to Kyūshū, but
even assuming someone could tell us which mountain he was on,
no one knows where on the mountain that particular camphor tree
was. We would have no way of finding it, would we?"

"There's the girl who saved him. We just have to find her."

"And how would we do that?"

"Oh, that's easy. She's sure to remember him—there can't have
been that many lieutenant colonels in the area. We just have to ask
around about the girl who saved a lieutenant colonel deep in the
mountains immediately after the defeat. We'll find her in no time."

The mother looked on somewhat suspiciously as Ineko was seized
with a somewhat odd enthusiasm. Then, as if to calm her, "I wonder
what your father ate then, during those days—three or four, however
many it was—when he was wandering, before he carved his name on
the tree. The horse, too. I can't imagine your father was in any state to
pack food before he rode up into the mountains. Don't you think?"

"You're right. It's so like you, Mother, that kind of sympathy," Ineko said. "Did you ever ask him? What he ate?"

"I never did. He didn't like to talk about his time in the mountains, so I tried not to ask. I knew he was searching for a place to commit suicide, after all. And as the years passed, the thought that even then, when he seemed to have lost himself, he still carved his rank in the bark—that really must have left a bitter taste in his mouth."

"That's so sad," Ineko said.

"Ah?" Ineko's mother replied, not with her voice but with her breath. For a moment she just stood there with her mouth open, saying nothing.

The word "sad" holds a vast range of meanings, and can be used in all sorts of situations. It is as ambiguous as any other word that describes a feeling, and among the most banal; yet when someone uses it unexpectedly it can hit hard, make a person emotional.

"It's good if you can savor the sadness, the loneliness of this world," Ineko's mother said eventually, then added, "Of course, it has to be just right. Some people go through life without experiencing even that much, and it can ..."

"Yes?" Ineko said as her mother searched for her next words. "Just right? You mean the right amount? Is there an appropriate amount of sadness?"

"For people like us, I mean."

"Oh?"

"I think this may be the right amount. Don't you?"

"Ah."

"When you've felt what it's like to be lonely, you realize there's no limit. You see how many people there are in the world who are so much sadder and more lonely than you. Compared to them, I don't think you and I are so badly off."

The sorrow Ineko's mother experienced as a military wife after the defeat, and that she and her daughter endured after Kizaki's unexpected death, went well beyond mere loneliness; and yet somewhere along the way the intensity of the emotion had been softened, and transformed, you might say, into a sense of forlornness that permeated their days together. So it seemed to the mother now as she looked back, prompted by Ineko's comment.

At the time, it must have been first nature to a military man like Ineko's father to carve that "Army Lieutenant Colonel" alongside his name in the bark of the camphor tree, even when he was lost to himself. As a commissioned officer who had graduated from the Military Academy and then from the Army Staff School, then climbed to the rank of colonel, Kizaki couldn't simply shed his rank on the day of the defeat. His attachment to that title had only been strengthened by the sense of inferiority he felt as a disabled officer with a fake leg and an assignment in the army that made it unclear whether or not he had really returned to active duty.

Now, more than a decade after the defeat, and in the wake of his death, it did indeed inspire a certain "loneliness" in his daughter and his wife to think of Kizaki carving his rank into that great tree. It was "lonely," too, to imagine the bitter taste Kizaki must have gotten in his mouth, years later, whenever he cast his thoughts back to all that he had done.

Ineko and her mother had both tried, all this time, to avoid bringing up either story: how Kizaki had vanished into the mountains after the defeat, or how he and his horse had tumbled from the cliff into the sea and died. Ineko and her mother of course had been thinking of these things when their conversation turned to the topic of loneliness, yet even now a substantial gap, a sizeable body of missing information, separated Ineko's use of the word "lonely" from her mother's. Still, they understood each other. Ineko's words had caught her mother off guard, and Ineko felt that her mother's had come from nowhere, but neither—feeling the other's words seep into her own individual loneliness—had been inclined to press. They could perhaps have spoken at greater length about how appropriate their loneliness was, in the context of the world around them, but they refrained even from this. Echoing her mother, Ineko settled into an acknowledgment that they lived with a suitable amount of loneliness, and that it was better that way.

"You know, Ineko," her mother said, her tone more formal than before. "I don't see any link between your blindness to the ping-pong ball and your father's inability to remember his wandering in the mountains. I don't think there's anything there, really—nothing hereditary. I just happened to think of your father, that's all. That's why I mentioned him."

"Oh?" Ineko seemed distracted, as if her mind were elsewhere and she hadn't really heard her mother's somewhat defensive comment.

Ineko's mother, meanwhile, had remembered something altogether different—something so peculiar it made her blush. She had heard it from the widow of a commissioned officer who had died in the war. A friend had invited the woman to a beauty parlor where men did all the work—there was even a male manicurist. It was amazing, she said, how much it helped her forget her stress. Ineko's mother had no idea why she had thought of that now.

Ineko herself was calling up an image of the young woman who had stumbled across her father in the mountains and saved him, kept him alive. Ineko no longer believed in her, that girl her mother had described as a sprite in the service of a god. Something in her mother's tone had suggested that she, too, had her doubts. But when she was younger, Ineko had been sure she existed. That young woman was constantly before her, vividly present. She inhabited Ineko. And Ineko herself was that young woman. Ineko felt that way from the time she was a child until yesterday. And still, having that image of the young woman in her mind's eye felt quite natural, even now that she had stopped believing.

Earlier, when Ineko had suggested in a loud and aggressive tone that she and her mother go search for the girl in Kyūshū, she had not intended any sarcasm toward her parents, or meant to ridicule them. She had spoken in earnest. True, she had come to believe the young woman was an illusion, perhaps a fiction her father had invented, but that didn't change the fact that that young woman had lived inside Ineko throughout her girlhood, and when the notion of setting out to find that young woman first occurred to Ineko, and when she proposed it to her mother, the young woman had in fact become somewhat more real. Oddly, underlying that strengthened sense of her reality was at the same time an increased anxiety about the possibility that she was a fiction. Her mother's evident unwillingness to accompany her up into the mountains of Kyūshū to hunt for the young woman and the camphor tree left Ineko feeling dissatisfied, it was true, but also relieved.

It had been quite a while since they last talked about Ineko's father's disappearance into the mountains following Japan's surrender, about "that day," so her mother had recounted the story as if she had never told it before; but for Ineko it was already a vivid memory—in fact, her first memory. In her innocence, Ineko had never thought to question the notion of a heavenly being, a maiden or a sprite who served a god, but there was no way to know exactly when the young woman had become Ineko, had come to inhabit her. Most likely it was soon after she first heard the story.

Little Ineko and the young woman hadn't been the same age, of course. Even as a small child, Ineko was aware of that. And so in her mind the young woman was simultaneously a little girl and a young woman. She wore the same clothes most women did at the time, a dark blue top with splashes of white paired with women's work pants, but the white splashes were special—each formed a cross. Those white crosses were clearer in Ineko's mind than any of the young woman's other attributes. Her face was Ineko's own, of course, but she was somewhat too mysterious and idealized to be described as identical, and from one day to the next her features could be more or less well defined, and sometimes underwent subtle changes.

That young woman met her unfortunate end, in Ineko's mind, when Ineko's father died. Ineko felt she herself had killed her father, because they had been riding together, side by side, when he fell from the cliff. Hard as she tried, she couldn't persuade herself that she was blameless. It was inevitable that the young woman would vanish from within her. That young woman had given Ineko's father his life; Ineko had killed him. It would be an exaggeration to say that the starkness of that opposition had led Ineko to deny the woman's existence, but it made it very painful to call her image to mind. In any event, Ineko was too distraught after her father's death to give her any thought.

Before long, though, the young woman was resurrected in Ineko's heart, and she began to find peace in her reappearance—more so, even, than in any hopes of her dead father's return. The young woman was just an illusion, after all, a comforting dream. She had never inspired in Ineko any terrible pangs of guilt. It was easy to say that the young woman had rescued her father, and that Ineko herself had killed him, but was any of this really true? Perhaps the young woman hadn't saved her father. Perhaps Ineko hadn't killed him. Either way, since her father's death the notion that that young woman had saved him was attended by a certain lonely nostalgia distinct from whatever it was she had felt before he died.

"It's entirely different," Ineko's mother said, pressing the point home. "His wandering in the mountains and your getting dizzy during the ping-pong game."

"It never occurred to me to compare them," Ineko replied. "You're the one who brought all that up, as if one thing reminded you of the other."

"Yes, that's true," Ineko's mother mumbled. "At any rate, the ball was only gone for a moment, right?"

"And only the ball was gone. I could still see everything else."

"It only seemed that way to you. You couldn't see anything else, either—your eyes were on the ball, and it all happened so suddenly ... isn't it kind of hard to say whether or not you could see anything else?"

"Not at all. I couldn't see the ball, but I returned it."

"But that's ..."

"It's not like that other time, Mother."

"What other time?"

"When I fainted while I was riding, and I couldn't see anything at all. Just for a moment, of course." Ineko was talking about her father's accident.

"That ..." Ineko's mother said, avoiding the topic. "You can't compare that to your ping-pong game, you really can't."

"No. But I remember it."

"You remembered a lot," Ineko's mother said, as if it were a joke. "Anyway, how are you feeling? There's more color in your face now than before, when you first got back."

"Is there? I haven't been feeling bad. Not since I got home."

"You certainly were pale."

"I was scared, that's all."

Ineko kept insisting she had stopped seeing the ping-pong ball, and her tone left no doubt that she believed this is what had happened. But her mother couldn't accept that. Ineko had just been so focused on the ball that it was the only thing that *seemed* to have vanished. There was nothing strange in that. Ineko's refusal to listen when her mother suggested this conveyed a sense of the terror she had felt during the few moments when she couldn't see the ball. You couldn't make light of something like that; but then what *could* you make of it? Maybe Ineko felt that the terror that had come over her then couldn't be shared. Suspecting that this might be the case, Ineko's mother gazed at Ineko—less at her face than at her form. Her daughter's shoulders and knees seemed less tense than before.

"Lie down for a bit, take it easy," Ineko's mother said. "I'll get dinner ready."

"I can't eat," Ineko said. "I can't eat." By the time she'd said that, she was covering her mouth, fighting a sudden urge to vomit. Her throat tightened; her eyes grew red and moist.

The mother hurriedly rubbed Ineko's back. "Are you all right?"

"I'm fine. It's okay." She was breathing the way people do at such times. "I don't know what came over me, just at the mention of dinner."

"You're exhausted. You should get some rest."

"It's okay." Ineko's mother was still massaging Ineko's back; now Ineko took her mother's hand in hers and brought it around to her chest. "I feel calmer looking at the camellias. I can see them just fine, all those flowers, and they don't seem to be swaying, or moving around."

"Yes?" Ineko's mother said, taken aback at those last words, but she decided not to ask what Ineko meant.

She saw the flowers blooming just as they were, neither swaying nor moving. That was only natural, so why would she bother to say it? Did the flowers' stillness comfort Ineko, help her feel at peace in the state she was in now?

Ineko's mother, too, turned and gazed out at the camellias. The flowers were absolutely still. They weren't swaying, no breeze was blowing. And of course flowers don't move around—they never leave the place where they bloom. From the time a flower blossoms to the time it drops, it remains in the same position on the same branch. Thinking this made them seem even more motionless than before. The vivid red flowers seemed detached from their surroundings, brilliant spots hovering in midair, perhaps because the green of the leaves was so deep, even heavy; but as one stared at the flowers' neatly delineated redness, one began to feel a sense of pity for them, emerging from the impression of loveliness they first conveyed. Ineko's mother couldn't remember ever having pitied a flower before. Perhaps she did when she was little, but if she had she couldn't remember. Ineko, though, had sometimes felt sorry for flowers when she was little, they had noticed that, and evidently her heart still moved in that way. Still, Ineko's mother had trouble understanding the fear that had prompted Ineko's unthinking comment, since fear was surely what it was, that the flowers didn't look as if they were swaying, or moving. The four or five camellias in the garden were already beginning to take on the colors of a late-autumn dusk.

Ineko's mother often remembered that day, back when Ineko was in her second year of high school. It was the first time Ineko had ever shared with her mother the terror of being unable to see something. Over time, the doubts she had harbored about Ineko's explanation had faded, until she came to accept that it had indeed happened precisely as Ineko said—that she had seen everything else, but not the ball. Presumably there were times during any ping-pong match when the ball moved faster than the eye could follow, but that wasn't relevant in this case: the ball she didn't see should have been visible.

"Did Ineko ever tell you about the time she stopped seeing a ping-pong ball during a game?" Ineko's mother asked Kuno.

"Ping pong?" Kuno looked confused. "No, she never said anything about ping-pong."

"Ah." The mother fell silent. She stared at a sliding door that led out into the hall. The rectangles of paper didn't look all that old, but the paper seemed thin and of inferior quality. They hadn't been stretched tight enough, either. These paper-paneled doors were exactly what you would expect to find in a run-down country town.

"What about ping-pong?" Kuno asked. "Does Ineko play?"

"She used to, way back when."

"When was that?"

"Until her second year of high school."

"That's not so long ago," Kuno said. He almost smiled, but didn't. "She's never mentioned ping-pong."

"Maybe she didn't want to talk about it."

"Why wouldn't she? Though in fact, she seems to have an aversion to talking about the past. She almost never does. That's struck me before, and I've wondered about it. Sharing memories is one of the great joys of being in love, don't you think?"

"You two are hardly old enough to be sharing memories."

"That's not true. Everyone has memories, lots of them—from when they were babies, or from their childhood, things that were enjoyable or sad, funny things, blunders. Everyone has an endless supply. And however trivial it may be, however minor, when Ineko tells me a story like that I listen in a way no one else ever will. The story enters me as love. If she tells me about some silly incident from when she was little, it's like a lullaby. It doesn't have to be anything big, any sort of confession—when you're in love, you get used to sharing even the most ordinary memories, and in the most casual way. Don't you think that's true?"

"I guess," Ineko's mother murmured, so quietly it wasn't even a reply.

"I'm fascinated to learn even the tiniest, most inconsequential things about Ineko before I knew her." Kuno looked at Ineko's mother. "And now here we are, Mother, you and I, unexpectedly spending the night together at this inn."

"It certainly is unexpected, isn't it?"

"We won't be able to sleep tonight—not after leaving Ineko in that awful clinic. If we can't sleep anyway, I wouldn't mind staying up all night hearing new stories about Ineko."

"That's kind of you."

Suddenly, Ineko's mother got up, opened the sliding door, and stepped into the hall.

"What is it?" Kuno called.

"Oh, nothing. When I went into the hall earlier I opened the curtain to look at the ocean. I thought I might have forgotten to close it, that's all."

The curtain was closed. Ineko's mother pulled it back a bit and stood facing the water.

"You see something?" Kuno asked, still sitting in the room.

"Nothing. The stars. Come see for yourself."

Kuno got up and walked over. "Lots of stars. The ocean is so calm," he said dully.

"Nothing in this view would tell us where we are," Ineko's mother said. "There seems to be nothing out there but the dark night."

"And yet we'll probably never forget this night, or this inn."

Returning to his spot on the floor, Kuno tried again. "Mother, tell me a story about Ineko, please. Anything you like."

"When you ask like that ... nothing comes to mind."

"You could start with her birth."

"Her birth?" Ineko's mother said, as if she doubted her ears. "You mean her actual birth, when I gave birth to her? Isn't it a bit odd for you to ask about that, Mr. Kuno? You're crazy, really."

"Perhaps, but that's what I'd like. To start from her birth."

"I'd prefer not to. I didn't see it, you know—what happened when I was giving birth. It's not the kind of thing you can talk about just because someone wants you to."

"Ah."

"Is Ineko so reluctant to talk about herself?" Ineko's mother asked. "To you, too?"

"So it seems."

"Really? Reluctant enough that you feel she isn't entirely comfortable with you?"

"No, that's not what I mean. I just want her to tell me more."

"I'm happy to hear that, but then maybe you're also being a bit greedy. People don't usually share every little thing about themselves, do they, even with a lover? That doesn't necessarily mean they're hiding things."

"Of course I can't know absolutely everything about Ineko, but if I could, that's how much I'd like to know. Everything."

"You know all about her, Mr. Kuno," Ineko's mother said forcefully. "That's how it seems to me. There's no question. You know as much about Ineko as any person could ever know about another, don't you think? You know her in a way no two men, or women, could ever know one another—the way a man and a woman do when they're in love."

"I'm aware of that. I was talking about deeper things, though—or maybe sometimes they could be incredibly slight things. The pleasure of listening to her go on about all the silly little things she remembers."

"And now she's sick. You saw more of her sickness than anyone."

"Let's not talk about that," Kuno said. "Not until tomorrow."

"Tomorrow?"

"Can't you forget that until tomorrow?"

"Ineko shared all her memories of her father's accident, I'm sure?"

"Memories? I'd say that's a bit too gentle a word. I doubt I'll ever heal the wounds she's suffered from that, even if I spend my whole life trying."

"Surely she's told you everything else, too? All the major events in her life so far? Though you say she doesn't like to talk about the past."

"I said that in part because I feel guilty, actually. When she's with me, when ... it's a bit awkward to have to talk about this, but when she and I are so close that we're almost joined, so to speak, and then for whatever reason, just like that, I become invisible to her—her terror of these episodes is just too cruel, it really is. And since it's my fault, I see it as a sin on my part. It's true it's an illness, but it's me who brings the attacks on. Naturally, my first thought was that she must have an extreme aversion to me, that she detests me, but it turns out that wasn't it, the episodes seem to be brought on by love, and that just breaks my heart. Still, there's no denying that I'm guilty of a sin."

"That isn't true." Ineko's mother shook her head. "Only think of that pong-pong-ball story—she'd never told you about that."

Just then, they heard the sound of the bell.

"Ah, it's nine o'clock. The nine o'clock bell," Kuno said.

"The nine o'clock bell," Ineko's mother repeated, looking over at the sliding doors beyond which lay the ocean. Kuno turned, too. Not because the tolling seemed to be coming from there, but because Ineko's mother had opened those doors and stepped out into the hallway when the six o'clock bell was ringing, and lifted the curtain to gaze out at the water.

"I wonder who's ringing it this time," Kuno said, concentrating on the sound. "Probably not Ineko."

The bell rang a second time. The evening was silent in this country town, and perhaps because they had the whole second floor of this dreary inn to themselves, the long, lingering hum of the bell seemed always on the verge of fading into nothing, but never did. Even when it finally ended it seemed not to have ended. It was as if the sound, ceasing, were still drifting about in the room, in the air, only in some other form. Then the bell was struck a third time.

"It sounds more settled," Kuno said. "It's not a madman striking it. This must be how it sounds when someone from the clinic does it, someone who knows what they're doing."

"We've settled down ourselves now, that's why. Because we're sitting and listening."

"They said at the clinic that they ring the bell at nine to help turn the patients' thoughts toward sleep. The town lets them do it because the sound is so tranquil, so peaceful."

The woman from the inn came to lay out their bedding. Presumably it was the bell that prompted her. When she began arranging the two futons next to each other, Kuno told her to put one in the next room. Ineko's mother sat motionless. Before the woman had finished in the other room, the bell at Jōkōji has ceased its ringing.

"How many times was that?" Kuno asked.

"I'm afraid I wasn't counting," Ineko's mother replied. "I'm sure they're done striking it, but somehow it seems as if it could go on ringing, don't you think?"

"We should have gone to see the bell. The doctor said they would have Ineko strike it at three, so you would think we'd have asked to see it. I can't imagine why it didn't occur to us. If we'd gone, we could have had an image in our minds as we listened at three, and six, and now again at nine."

"It must be quite old. Otherwise the military would have made them give it up during the war," Ineko's mother said. She hesitated a moment, then went on. "Mr. Kuno, did Ineko ever tell you about the white heron at Emperor Nintoku's tomb?"

"A white heron at a tomb?" Kuno eyed Ineko's mother. "No, I haven't heard about that."

"Oh, it's nothing, really. When she was in high school, Ineko went on a trip to Kansai with some friends, and they visited Emperor Nintoku's tomb. It's very large, as you know. A huge mound, covered in trees. And above all that green—that broad, thick expanse of foliage—there was a flock of white herons. So many you can't imagine. Ineko was so moved by that—the herons made more of an impression on her than anything else on that trip."

"I see."

"I thought of that just now, that story about Emperor Nintoku's herons, as I was listening to the bell."

"Ineko never told me that," Kuno said. "I wonder why the bell reminded you of that."

"No reason, I just remembered. You never know what will come to you."

"A flock of white herons over a mass of green would certainly be impressive," Kuno said, looking as if he were trying to imagine the scene. "I suppose some of the birds must have been resting on the trees, while others were flying around up above."

"Yes, she said some were flying. It was an incredible number of herons."

"You're lucky to see a sight like that once in your life. Even if the herons lived there, on the tomb."

"She asked me to go visit the tomb with her, so she could show me the herons, but we haven't gotten around to it yet. I wonder if they are still there."

"What kind of birds live in the woods around Jōkōji, do you think?"

"I couldn't say."

"Maybe the woods are full of birds with welcoming songs, just as the banks of Ikuta River are covered in dandelions. Those very woods, inhabited by madmen …"

Ineko's mother didn't reply to this, so Kuno fell silent for a time, too.

"I don't believe I ever asked Ineko about the trees on Emperor Nintoku's tomb, but I'm sure there must have been some pines. Sometimes trees can seem a bit frightening, when they're too dense, or when they get too old or too big, but I think in most cases trees tend to put people in a tender mood. Grass, too. And those dandelions along the river, and the woods around Jōkōji."

"Yes, I agree."

"That word 'tender' reminds me to tell you something, Mr. Kuno," Ineko's mother squinted her eyes slightly, then glanced up at Kuno's face. "Perhaps it's cruel of you to be as tender as you are to Ineko."

"Cruel?" Kuno replied, startled.

"From a woman's perspective, there's something cruel in a man's tenderness. A woman told me that once, an old friend. I suppose the words have stuck with me because they were so unexpected. They caught me off guard—I was so taken aback I felt like something in my chest had toppled over, but when I thought it over later on, I realized there was nothing strange in it at all. It happens all the time, that a man's tenderness has a cruel effect on a woman."

"That's a cruel thing to say to me. Terribly cruel."

"Is it? I meant it as an apology."

"An apology? Well, that sounds just as cruel. Like you're telling me not to love Ineko. That you want me to stop loving her."

"That's not quite right," Ineko's mother said quietly, refusing to be drawn in by Kuno's agitated tone. "Tell me, Mr. Kuno. If I fall asleep before you, aren't you planning to sneak out and go up to the Ikuta Clinic, to bring Ineko back? You are, aren't you."

"Tonight? No, that hadn't occurred to me. Tomorrow, maybe."

"Then I can sleep easy tonight?"

"I doubt you'll get any sleep. Just like Ineko, who won't be able to sleep at the clinic, lying there surrounded by all those crazies. She doesn't have a private room, after all. She's not at Emperor Nintoku's tomb, amidst all that greenery. She might imagine the white herons, but it will be an illusion. Who knows, maybe she'll escape on her own, even without me going to fetch her. There are no bars to keep her in." Kuno got to his feet as he was speaking. Ineko's mother watched him. He began pacing up and down.

"Mr. Kuno, would you please go to the other room," Ineko's mother said, a stern note in her voice. "I want very badly to lie down. Neither Ineko nor I slept a wink last night."

"All right. Get some rest."

"I wonder why you were born, Mr. Kuno, and why you and Ineko ended up together."

"What? How can you be so negative about everything? Or maybe you don't intend for it to sound that way, maybe you genuinely meant it as a question?"

"Perhaps I said it because I'm so exhausted that my head isn't right."

"Maybe its my head that isn't right. But even if it isn't, that hasn't made me fall for someone I should never have loved. Maybe deep down in your heart you want me to break up with Ineko, but if I ever did leave her, something awful would happen. I really feel that way. Something terrible, I'm sure of it."

"That's not a very tender thing to say."

"I don't know if it's tender or not, but I think that sort of feeling is what lies at the core of tenderness. Only ... no, tenderness isn't the word. I mean something more intense."

"Mr. Kuno. When you lie with her, she stops seeing you. You know that."

"That isn't a denial—her denying me. What is it? Help me think about that, Mother."

"Will thinking make it clear? Here on our futons, with our hearts calm?"

"Is that how you see it?" Kuno walked into the next room. "Shall I close the doors?"

"Please do."

"Good night," Kuno said from the next room after he had slid the doors shut. There was a moment of silence. Then, "Mother?"

Perhaps because she could no longer see him, either his face or his body, she seemed to detect a certain pleading note in his voice.

"Good night," Ineko's mother replied, her own tone somewhat more friendly. "Are you in bed already?"

"I was just debating whether to sit on the futon or get in under the covers."

"Oh. Why is that?"

"Have you, Mother?"

"Me? I guess you could say I was wondering what to do, too, though I wasn't thinking in any real sense of the word. I just don't feel like I'll be able to sleep."

"I wouldn't imagine you could."

"I'm tired enough. Not having slept last night."

"I think you should lie down."

"I will. You, too, Mr. Kuno."

"I'm still mulling over which is best. Is it easier to set my heart free, to let it fly through the sky, if I sit with my feet tucked under me, my back straight? Or will it be easier if I lie down and let all the strength drain from body. How can I make my heart like the sound of the bell at Jōkōji as it flies through the emptiness?"

"Toward Ineko, you mean?"

"Yes," Kuno replied without hesitating. "The sound of the bell we heard earlier, though, Mother—it's gone now. We can listen as hard as we like, but we won't hear it anymore. Could it be, though, that our hearing just isn't sharp enough? I remember reading in some book that our ears are designed to hear sounds within a certain range. There are lots of animals who hear better than we do. Of course, animals are living creatures just like us, so there must be limits on what they can hear, too. Or maybe certain animals have a sixth sense, or a seventh or some other number, that lets them feel inaudible sounds?"

"I've heard that. And not just sounds — they have some sort of instinct that warns them beforehand of natural disasters and other calamities."

"Humans probably had a sixth sense like that, too, in ancient times, at the very beginning. You know, I often wonder about the effect on people's ears of constant, unending noise like you get in a place like Tokyo, the terrible racket of the city."

"Our ears have gotten duller, of course. Just like our feelings have been blunted."

"I'm sure that's true. And yet people in the country seem less attentive to sounds, don't you think? That's the impression I get from their expressions, at any rate."

"I doubt it's only sounds that make their expressions that way," Ineko's mother said, putting an end to that line of discussion. Then she launched into a new topic. "I remember something else. Kizaki went on a trip to Europe once, he was gone for four months or so, and when he came back, whenever he looked out the window of a train at all the Japanese people walking on the platforms and the streets, he'd say that somehow they just didn't look right in their Western clothing. Why do they have to swagger like that? They hurry along in the most weary manner, or throw themselves back in their seats like they're determined not to let anyone get the best of them. Sometimes when we were on the train together he'd start chuckling to himself, and when I wanted to know what was so funny, he'd ask why everyone was trying so hard: he'd point out how stern their expressions were — or maybe less stern than pathetic. That's how it struck him. The line from the shoulder to the collar on men's jackets was almost always wrong, he said. He was talking about people in Tokyo, before the war. I'm sure it's a little different now, though I don't see that things have changed all that much. Now when I take the train and I see the people out on the platform, I remember Kizaki saying those things and it makes me feel sort of sad, sort of wretched."

"From remembering Ineko's father, or from seeing how Japanese men are dressed?"

"Both. I can't separate them."

All this while, they were talking through the sliding doors. She hadn't heard anything that suggested Kuno was lying down. Was he sitting crosslegged on his futon? Or more properly, kneeling with his feet tucked beneath his legs? Most likely the latter, she thought.

"Something else has just come to me. This one's odd, too," Ineko's mother said. "Once when Kizaki went to a department store in London, he saw an outfit that was both elegantly tailored and extremely gallant-looking, so he called the clerk over and told him he wanted to buy it. And the clerk said, 'This is a lady's riding costume.' The top of the pants had seemed kind of wide and the bottom of the legs quite tight. That was why."

"Hmm."

"He should have bought it. If he had known Ineko would become an equestrian, he could have gotten it for her. A nice, attractive riding costume from the country that invented riding. Kizaki used to say that sometimes—he regretted that he hadn't purchased it his whole life. It's odd, though, he was a rider himself, and yet he couldn't recognize the stylish outfit for the lady's riding costume it was. Perhaps because he was a military man, and a boor. I suppose it might have been different if it had been hanging up."

"Hmm."

Kuno listened intently to her digressions, as long as they involved Ineko.

"I'll buy Ineko one if we ever visit London together, once we're married. I'll do that."

"You know she doesn't ride anymore."

Kuno didn't know how to respond. Realizing that her tone had suddenly become rather harsh, Ineko's mother continued, "He didn't buy that outfit, but he did get some riding gear for himself. He treasured those things, and took good care of them."

Kuno wondered whether Kizaki was using the things he had brought back from England when he tumbled from that cliff in Izu, but of course he didn't ask. Instead, he just repeated what he'd said earlier.

"I think it might help if Ineko and I rode together. I'll take lessons, and we'll take a trip to Izu together, on horseback. That's my plan. Not like criminals returning to the scene of the crime—not at all like that. It will serve as an offering. People often go out on the ocean and scatter flowers on the waves for people who died at sea, right? They steer the boat to a spot that seems close enough to where it happened, since there are no markers on the water. And the flowers scatter, and they keep moving, too, drifting about on the waves."

"Yes. Though in his case, we know the location. You could find that big rock."

"Rocks last a thousand years, ten thousand years."

"They do. It makes no difference to a big rock like that if one or two poor men like Kizaki break their bodies on its face. Humans wouldn't leave so much as a scratch. And our world is just the same, wouldn't you say? Whether he lived or died, it made no difference— Japan and the rest of the world have gone on just as they would have anyway, from that day to the present. Nothing has changed. Ineko and I grieved, of course, we suffered, but what does that matter to the world? How many people even know of our sorrow, our suffering?"

"I do."

"Yes, that's right. You're the one," said Ineko's mother with a chuckle, her tone surprisingly cheerful. "There is one person who knows, then, that's true. And I know you're on our side, whatever may happen. There's nothing more precious than a person like that— someone you can count on absolutely. Even parents and children, even spouses or lovers sometimes stop being there for each other. Personally, I could only ever put complete faith in someone I was sure I could rely on no matter how awful or low or hateful my actions had been, someone who would definitely support me. What point is there in faulting people for moral failings, flaws in their character, when you're in a relationship with them?" For seem reason, Ineko's mother had grown agitated.

"I'm here for you. And that means a hundred other people, a thousand, are here for you, too. I can assure you of that."

"It's kind of you to say so. Of course, I'd be lying if I said I see things the same way, but I'll allow myself to be persuaded."

"Even that rock—we could smash it to pieces, just like that. A bit of gunpowder is all it would take. People destroy great mountains all the time, one after the next."

"That's true, of course, but even if we smashed them all, the Alps and the Himalayas and all the rest, even if we filled in all the great oceans, nature would still be nature, solemn and indestructible. Human lives are over so quickly. A little plate can easily outlive a human. Life goes on, from a child to the child's child, but for how long? The chain ends fairly soon."

"I don't let that concern me. All I want is to be happily married to Ineko."

"Happily married? Well, I'm sorry she's like that."

"You and I, we feel differently about what it is to be … like that."

"You're the one who feels how frightening it is, though, how hateful—more so even than I do, as her mother. Wouldn't you agree? How she must shake, how she must wail and writhe when you hold her, and she stops seeing you. Forgive me for saying this, but that's not what it's like when that special joy comes over a woman. Ineko loses her mind, doesn't she?"

"I find her more adorable than ever, then. More loveable."

"You're an odd one," Ineko's mother said, as casually as she could manage. "She's gotten into your heart so much you're getting weird yourself. I can't let this go on."

"There's no need to put her in a madhouse."

"Ineko will die if it goes on the way it has. Her life will end, Mr. Kuno."

"She'll grow weak and die, you mean? Or do you think she'd kill herself?"

"Both. You can't deny either possibility. Perhaps it's because I'm her mother, I don't know, but I sense something, somehow, in her heart or maybe her body, something we can't afford to ignore. It's made me scared. I simply can't ignore it."

"Ah," Kuno said glumly.

After that, silence reigned for a time on both sides of the sliding doors. The flimsy panels, covered in cheap paper that was now worn and yellowing, without a picture or even a pattern to liven them up, their frames shoddily lacquered, were like a heavy wall between the rooms, and yet at the same time it was almost as if they weren't there at all.

"Mr. Kuno, why don't you lie down," Ineko's mother said then.

"Ah. My heart feels more settled when I sit, like it might make its way to Ineko. Priests sit like this, after all. When they want to focus their hearts, fill them with prayer."

"You're putting your hands together, aren't you?"

"What? You can see me?"

"I can tell."

"Oh?"

"You're not an ascetic. Your heart will move more freely if you lie down and relax."

"All right, I will." Kuno didn't protest. "And you, Mother?"

"I'm about ready to lie down, too. I'd probably distract you if I stayed up," Ineko's mother said. "We can talk a little more as we lie here."

"All night long, if you like."

"The whole night?"

"We'll end up talking until morning, I'm sure."

"I don't think I could take that," Ineko's mother said, a plaintive note in her voice. With that, she began getting ready for bed: undoing her obi, folding her haori and kimono. She tried to do all this as silently as she could, but she knew Kuno could hear her in the next room. The thought made her movements a little more awkward than they had been until then.

She hesitated for a moment, wondering whether she should remove the cloth she wore wrapped around her waist beneath her under-kimono, or leave it on and put the yukata the inn had provided on over it. At home, she would have taken it off. She was used to sleeping without it, and hardly ever stayed at an inn.

"It doesn't matter," she said, so softly she was less speaking to herself than thinking aloud. "There's no reason to feel I shouldn't tonight. And at my age . . . ."

So what if there was a young man on the other side of those sliding doors—he was her daughter's lover. Kuno's mind was filled with thoughts of Ineko, she was like hot water brimming inside him; he didn't even regard Ineko's mother as a woman. There must be something wrong with her, though, thought Ineko's mother, that she was even thinking about how he saw her.

There was no reason whatsoever for her to be thinking of Kuno as she debated whether or not to remove her slip. If she was worried that it might get cold here on the shore, even in this warm town where the dandelions started blooming in midwinter, she could simply have gone to sleep with it on. The yukata from the inn had been washed and starched, but it was starting to look a bit old. She didn't like the thought of wearing the fabric directly against her stomach or thighs. This aversion, which had come over her without any warning, led her to look down at the pure white piece of silk she had wrapped around her, from her waist down to her knees. White slips like this tended to get slightly soiled at the edge, but she took great care to prevent this, and changed hers constantly; frugal as she was in her day-to-day life, this was one of the few luxuries she countenanced. Every so often, it occurred to her that the white of this silk was unlikely to catch a man's fancy; that it was a color best suited to a widow like her.

Ineko's mother loosened the cord around the slip slightly to make herself more comfortable, but that was all. The presence of a young man in the next room and the well-worn look of the inn's yukata were what led her to question whether or not she ought to wear the slip, but when she lowered her eyes to the curves of her thighs under the white silk, she found herself thinking of her departed husband Kizaki. An image of him flicked up in her heart.

"The woman of forty will do everything for you. The woman of twenty nothing."

She heard these words quite clearly, spoken in Kizaki's voice. She had forgotten the title of the translation in which they appeared, but she remembered Kizaki calling to her when he encountered them, and then reading them aloud.

"That's Balzac. Balzac," he said. "You know his works better than I do, I'm sure, but I bet you don't know that quote. Let me read it again. *A woman of forty will do everything for you. A woman of twenty nothing.* How do you like that?"

"What do you mean? How do I like it?" Ineko's mother hadn't been able to share her husband's enthusiasm, and the phrase her husband had seemed so taken with struck her at first as a rather unremarkable aphorism.

Ineko's father had been to the West and for a military man he was fairly cultured, but the longer he spent in the militaristic atmosphere pervading the country in the years before the war and then during the war itself, the narrower his thinking had become. Sent reeling by the defeat, he gave himself up to the trends of the age, in part to distract himself from his grief at the defeat, though deep in his heart he rebelled against these new ways; and so, when he read works of literature or religion, he would get sucked in so easily it was almost silly. He had developed a habit of being so struck with admiration by famous passages and aphorisms and so on that he would call his wife over and read them to her.

It was only natural that Ineko's mother took this particular aphorism to be another instance of that habit.

"Doesn't it depend on the woman, how fully she devotes herself to the man she's with, and how well she takes care of him? I don't see that it has anything to do with age, whether she's forty or twenty," Ineko's mother had said. "I'm sure there must be women out there who do everything for their men when they are twenty, and then when they get to be forty refuse to do anything at all."

"When you put it in that commonsensical way, you weaken the impact of Balzac's phrase." Ineko's father had grown testy. "It's an unpleasant word game, taking something someone says and flipping it around like that."

"Men make women, and women are made by men. That's another one."

"What?" Ineko's father had seemed taken aback.

Amused, Ineko's mother had made another verbal leap. "You ought to make a women as you would like her to be made. I'm sure that would make the woman happy. A man who doesn't have it in him to make a woman into what he wants her to be isn't really a man."

Ineko's father looked at Ineko's mother, his eyes registering his puzzlement. He seemed startled that his wife had said something so out of character.

This was as far as the conversation had gone, but for some reason those Balzac lines that her husband had read aloud lingered in Ineko's mother's memory. She wasn't sure what to make of that quotation, since she hadn't questioned her husband about how Balzac had used them, what nuance he might have invested them with—if those words had been rooted in his own personal experiences, or had described a fictional character—and she herself had never read the book in which her husband had found them. She had the sense, though, that when her husband had encountered the aphorism, it had occurred to him that one day his own wife would be forty. Perhaps as a result, the words had touched him in some special way, or inspired in him an expectation, a hope. But by the time she thought of this, already four or five days had passed.

Back then, Kizaki would sink his teeth into Ineko's mother's breasts, or grab her hair and roughly shake her head, telling her, "I can't enjoy life's greatest delicacy! The best part!"

As he grew wilder, his voice would start to sound like a wail and Ineko's mother felt she might faint. She couldn't even cry.

"Please, calm down, be quiet—that would be so much better," she would have liked to say, but white with terror she didn't have the presence of mind to offer such wisdom. Before she could even try and comfort her husband, to soothe his nerves, he'd grow so rough it was really beyond the pale. You could say that as a soldier, the role he had played in the war had been no fault of his own, but it didn't matter; he flailed like this because "life's greatest delicacy" had been stolen from him less as heaven's punishment for the role he played in the war than as a castigation on a human scale.

For Ineko's mother, that phrase, "*A woman of forty will do everything for you*," was a revelation. And she succeeded in molding herself to it. All this meant was that she became a motherly prostitute, or acquired a prostitute-like motherliness—nothing many "women of twenty" wouldn't already have known about. But as far as Ineko's mother was concerned, it was a new experience.

It was because the words had been useful to Ineko's mother in that way that, looking down at the curve of her knees, she heard Kizaki's voice speaking them there in that cheap inn in Ikuta. Kizaki had died before she became a woman of forty. And now she was older than that. Her husband's life had ended before she had ever had an opportunity to do "everything" for him, and now before too long her own life would end as well. Sometimes Ineko's mother wondered what was included in that "everything"—just how much a woman could do for a man. *Everything* seemed to her limitless. Sometimes she felt she had been unable to do anything at all for her husband, and that pained her. Needless to say, this was more a sentimental game than anything else; deep in her heart, she felt had given as much as could be expected to her husband, and whatever her failings, they had been excused. There were times when she despised herself for a deviousness she regarded as typically feminine, or hated herself because her jealousy had played a part in his death, but she was well aware that as long as a woman lives she will find ways to justify all her actions, and to forgive herself for any sort of mistake. Occasionally, looking back, she would ask herself if this awareness might have made her a somewhat cold mother to Ineko.

"Time to sleep, Mr. Kuno," Ineko's mother called out, and quietly crept under the covers. "It really is time to lie down. Oh, they've given us hot water bottles."

"Have they? I don't need one."

"You don't? It's very nice to feel the warmth just beyond your feet. It's winter, after all, even in a town like this."

"Ah."

"You don't use hot water bottles or electric blankets in Tokyo, either, I guess?"

"No. Why do you ask?" Mr. Kuno seemed irked that Ineko's mother was talking about hot water bottles and so on.

Ineko's mother noticed, saying: "Ineko's feet are always cold, aren't they?"

Kuno couldn't suppress a little gasp at this. Perhaps because she was on the other side of the sliding doors, he seemed to detect a slightly flirtatious note in Ineko's mother's voice.

"I doubt they have hot water bottles at the clinic," Kuno said, returning to the topic on his own this time.

"Oh, I think they might. I bet they do. There are elderly people there, too, after all."

"That's true, there are … that strange old man …"

They stopped talking for a while.

Then Ineko's mother spoke again. "When it's this quiet, don't you feel as though you can still hear the sound of the bell, way off in the distance, in the sky above the ocean?"

"Maybe. I don't know."

"Do you remember, Mr. Kuno, how the temples were forced to turn in their bells during the war?"

"I heard about that. I have the feeling I may even have seen a big hanging bell being rolled along somewhere, though I could be imagining it."

"Yes. After the war, I remember seeing that too—a whole bunch of bells that had been left somewhere, thrown away. I assume they made the temples turn them in because they're made of iron, but then they couldn't use it."

"None of it—from the bamboo spears to the bells."

"Eighty percent of the bells in the entire country, I think it was, or maybe ninety. It's amazing when you think of it, because evidently there were about fifty thousand bells to start. I saw that total somewhere once, in something I read."

"Do you think Jōkōji got its bell back after the war?"

"Maybe they didn't have to turn it in," Ineko's mother said. "I have the feeling they didn't collect the older bells, from before the Edo period. There's a phrase, *tōne no sasu kane*—a bell with a distant ring. It's a nice way to describe the sound of an old bell, don't you think?"

"A distant ring. Yes, that's nice, and you could say that about this conversation, too."

"Don't be ridiculous—not this random chatter. And I don't have such a nice voice." Ineko's mother laughed. "It's a more elegant phrase than that."

"I wish our sounds carried far enough to reach Ineko, at the clinic. I'd like to stay up through this quiet night, until morning, talking that way with Ineko. A distant talk."

"Oh?" Ineko's mother murmured. "Perhaps I should be quiet, then."

"No, not at all. Whatever you may be saying, I can still have my distant talk with Ineko."

"It would be nice if you could."

"Mother, did you see the white dandelion blooming on the bank of Ikuta River?"

"A white dandelion? Is there such a thing?"

"I saw one blooming there, just one. You didn't see it?"

"No. I bet it's just another thing you saw—an illusion, like the white rat."

"That's not true. I saw the white rat and the white dandelion both, there's no doubt about that, right there on the river bank. I'll show you tomorrow morning, on our way to the clinic. I can't promise I'll be able to show you the rat, since rats move about, but I'm sure you'll see the dandelion. A dandelion isn't going to walk away."

"All right. I suppose the blossom is probably closed now."

"Huh," Kuno murmured, as if to himself. "Yes, I guess dandelions close their eyes when they go to sleep, too. Maybe that's why they bloom so long."

"There are all sorts of different flowers. Do you know the lines, *Enlightenment in the voice of the bamboo; radiance of heart in the peach blossom*? Ineko may not be enlightened by the dandelions here, or by the sound of bamboo leaves rustling in the wind, but it would be nice if she could find a certain radiance of the heart, as the phrase has it. And soon."

"Mother," Kuno said sharply. "Ineko's heart isn't dark. It isn't like that."

"Isn't it? I guess I'm wrong, then. Though I don't think achieving 'radiance of heart' is quite about that—it's not about bringing light to a heart cast in darkness. Of course, you can take those lines in all kinds of ways, too: the darkness of the heart, brightening the heart. If you're talking about a radiance of the heart in terms of the way or the dharma, that's quite a difficult thing to accomplish. I just mean making the heart bright. But it's not about making a dark heart bright. I don't think that Ineko has a dark heart, or a dark personality. And yet ..."

"And yet?" Kuno repeated.

Ineko's mother seemed to have gotten up from her futon quietly; Kuno saw above the screen that her room grew less light, then went dark. The mother had turned off the light hanging from the ceiling, and then switched off the one by her pillow as well. There was no lamp by Kuno's own pillow. He looked up at the naked bulb overhead. It was probably a forty-watt bulb, but the glass looked sooty, and it emitted only a feeble light.

"Shall I turn out the light over here, too?" Kuno asked. "You think you can sleep?"

"Yes ... and no. But you should go to sleep, Mr. Kuno."

"It's the same for me. Yes, and no."

"Oh dear. It's still early, though."

"Yes."

"I'm grateful for all your efforts today. Don't you feel it was a very, very long day?"

"Yes, I'm sure it must have been for you. You must be exhausted. You didn't get any sleep last night, and then you carried right on into today," Kuno said. "I can't really tell how I feel myself—whether this was a long day, or a short one."

"It's a very odd place we've found to sleep tonight, don't you think?"

"Perhaps. But neither of us is really concerned about whether or not we actually get any rest tonight as we are about Ineko, and whether or not she can sleep. Isn't that so?"

"Ineko's gone to sleep, I'm sure. The people at the clinic will have given her a sedative or a sleeping pill."

"What?" Kuno seemed taken aback by this. "You think they would do that?"

"It's a clinic, after all."

"I was imagining her drifting off and then dreaming of you or me—well, less a real dream than a sort of mixture of dreams and reality."

"I doubt the medicine lets her dream."

"Is that true?" Kuno said, his dissatisfaction evident in his tone. "I'd like her to dream."

"That would be too terrible for her. Think how desolate and lonely she'd feel when she woke up after a dream about you. It would be too much to bear."

She had a point. It was Ineko's first night at the madhouse. She was lying there in the dark, crazy women sleeping all around her. None of them were young and beautiful like her; they filled the air with the grimy old smell of the mad. Perhaps they snored, grinding their teeth, or talking in their sleep—and not the way other people did. The tatami had been stripped of their borders and felt puffy underfoot; the crazies had pulled at them so much that they had gotten nappy. Since it was winter there would be no owls hooting, but the wild-growing, now leafless oaks would emit a quiet creak each time the wind blew, no matter how softly. However lonely or forlorn she felt, she wouldn't be allowed to turn on a light for herself, or to get up and move around.

Still, Kuno hoped that Ineko would dream. If he slept himself, he was sure he would see her in his dreams. He couldn't help feeling, too, that Ineko was bound to dream, even if they'd given her enough sleeping pills to keep her from dreaming. He had the sense that Ineko was more inclined than most to dream.

Thinking these thoughts, Kuno stared up at the old naked bulb above his futon. He gazed at it so long that it blinded him, even though the illumination wasn't all that bright—and now he couldn't see anything else. Just then, a peach-colored arc appeared, stretched like a rainbow across his blurry field of vision.

"Ineko!" Kuno cried out.

When had that been—the time Ineko told Kuno that while she was looking at him, a pink rainbow-like arc had appeared before him. She had described that rainbow in the most lovely way. It was a collection of tiny bubbles. The bubbles were pink, and touched by a faint light. They moved about very slowly. Each bubble moved on its own, and yet there was nothing chaotic about the rainbow as a whole. Ineko had described it all in such lovely detail. The fact that the rainbow came so unexpectedly made the odd scene she described sound very lovely. And she had waited until she settled down to tell him.

"Ah! I can't see you, I can't see you!" she had shouted at first. She put her left hand to her forehead and blinked repeatedly. "Your shoulders are gone. Oh, and your mouth, and your chin."

From his mouth on down—his shoulders, his chest—Kuno had slowly faded away into nothing. And then, in the void he left behind, a vague arc had shimmered into view, gradually assuming the form of a pink rainbow made of bubbles. Ineko's terror was lessened somewhat by the wonder she felt at the sight of the rainbow.

Kuno and Ineko hadn't been embracing then. They were apart. Kuno was standing near the window. Ineko was sitting on a chair in the middle of the room. They were in Kuno's apartment. It was on the fourth floor. The window faced west, but the day was too cloudy for a typical late-autumn sunset; the gray sky made the window look dim. They hadn't thought to turn on the lights. The pink of the bubbly rainbow wasn't particularly intense, but it shone with a pale light that brightened the area around it. The impression it made on Ineko was both soft and sharp.

"You're riding a rainbow," Ineko said.

Kuno was standing, not in the rainbow, but beyond it. The rainbow hovered between the two of them, but much closer to Kuno than to her. Everything from his shoulders—in fact even from his mouth on down—had vanished into the rainbow. The rainbow-shaped band of bubbles looked as though it *ought* to be transparent, as though it shouldn't conceal what lay behind it, so it would have been quite natural for Ineko to be uneasy and frightened about her inability to see Kuno's body. But the odd beauty of the rainbow distracted her.

Kuno couldn't see the pink rainbow in front of him. He had no sense that he was riding on a pink rainbow, as if he were some sacred being not of this world, perched on a purple or multicolored cloud. He only knew about all this from what Ineko told him. He wasn't all that surprised by the vision, or the partial blindness, Ineko had experienced. Because several times already she had stopped seeing his body while they embraced.

Still, this was the first time she had stopped seeing him when they weren't together in that way. It seemed possible to Kuno that her so-magnosia had gotten worse. But neither of them were in a state of excitement, as they were when they lay together, and perhaps on account of the rainbow Ineko didn't tremble the way she did when he held her. She gazed in rapture at the rainbow and at the upper half of Kuno's face, her eyes seemingly all pupil.

"Is the rainbow still there?" Kuno asked after a few moments.

"Yes." Ineko spoke as if there were nothing odd in this, which Kuno found odd.

"Is it pretty?" Kuno asked, as gently as he could.

"Very pretty," Ineko replied, as if she were half dreaming and half awake. "So this is the kind of man you are. I feel I've understood you now."

"What kind of man am I?"

"The kind of man I'm seeing right now."

"I don't know what you're seeing. How do I look?"

"You don't need to know. You're not looking at yourself—it's me looking at you, and getting a sense of the kind of man you are."

"Is this the first time you've seen this sort of rainbow, Ineko? Including the times when you weren't with me?"

"Yes, it is," Ineko said simply. "This is the first time."

Kuno began to think Ineko wasn't her usual self. He had to call her usual self back. What would happen to her if he allowed her to go on seeing these illusions too long?

"Seeing you like this, I realize I shouldn't be doing those things we do," Ineko said, seemingly to herself. And then she blushed.

Kuno was shocked. "Ineko."

"Yes?"

Kuno rose and walked over to Ineko, grasped her shoulders, and shook her. "There's no rainbow here."

"I know that," Ineko said, as if it had nothing to do with her. "But it was lovely."

"Put your arms around my shoulders. I'm here, right?"

"You are."

Kuno hugged Ineko more tightly and kissed her. Ineko's soft lips were cold.

"Is the rainbow there?"

"It's gone."

The thought occurred to Kuno that now Ineko wasn't only losing sight of him, she was also seeing pink rainbows which weren't there. This was more than what had happened before. She said this was the first time such a thing had ever happened, so perhaps this was a second illness, added to the first. Ineko herself might take comfort in this; but it only added to Kuno's grief.

Kuno lifted Ineko in his arms and gently lay her down.

"You could see me? I didn't vanish?" he asked afterwards.

"Yes, I could see you," Ineko answered in the faintest of whispers.

Ineko didn't stop seeing Kuno every time he slept with her. Sometimes she did, sometimes she didn't. Neither of them could tell what made her stop seeing him, or what kept that from happening.

Ineko would cry out and start trembling when she stopped seeing him. There were times when she would cling to him, and times when she would push him away. Ineko herself could not say what made her do one thing or the other. It was rare for her to thrust Kuno away with all her might; when he held her roughly, she would drown all the more deeply in his arms. And yet there were times when she pushed him away. He would stay where she had pushed him. "Can you see me?" he would ask, his voice shaking. "Are you able to see my whole body?" He felt then as if he was tumbling down into a dark valley.

Ineko didn't keep her eyes open the whole time. Her eyelids would close on their own. That was okay. But it was altogether different when she blurted out, "Ah, I can't see! I can't see you!" and then asked him to cover her eyes, and he did so, pressing down on her eyelids with his hand or his lips. She couldn't see Kuno either way, but when her eyes closed of their own accord she felt as if she could still see him, and when he shut her eyes for her after she had stopped seeing him, then she felt that she really wasn't able to see him.

Translator's afterword

ALMOST FIFTY YEARS have passed since Yasunari Kawabata died; a century has gone by since his first story appeared in a school literary magazine. Time has not blunted the weird, unsettling shock of his fiction, as the publication of *Dandelions*—his last, unfinished novel—so amply demonstrates. It has, however, left us with an image of Kawabata as a writer who would surely have struck many of his contemporaries as subtly off.

It is difficult, confronted by a neat row of translated books, or by the thirty-seven blue-green volumes of Kawabata's collected works in Japanese, to imagine what it must have been like to follow his career as an author in real time—to read his novels as they were published. In part this is because he lived in a world so different from the one we inhabit today: born six months before the end of the nineteenth century, he was in many ways a creature not simply of the twentieth century, but of its first half. Beyond this, though, there is the mundane and yet in some sense more intractable issue of publication history: the manner in which Kawabata first presented his novels to readers. More often than not, he would give out just a little at a time, serializing, often in different publications, what might at first appear to be discrete stories, only to weave them together, after much rewriting and reorganizing, into a loosely structured novel. *Snow Country*, which is often considered Kawabata's masterpiece, was first published in seven installments over two and a half years, from 1935 to 1937, in five different magazines. In 1948, Kawabata published an expanded "final version" incorporating new material he had begun offering to magazines in 1942. And even this turned out to be merely another stage in the novel's maturation: Kawabata revised the text four more times between 1948 and 1972, and after he died they found, near his desk, an abbreviated version that he had copied out by hand, altering the calligraphic style to suit the prose in each scene.

Kawabata was, one might say, as much a revisionist as he was a novelist: there was always the possibility that a work of his might be unfinalized, reopened, transformed. The ending you knew might not be the ending; there might not be an ending. In this sense, one could perhaps say that *Dandelions*, the most obviously incomplete of Kawabata's novels, captures with greater permanence and finality something that was always present in his art. Its provisionality offers us a clearer vision of Kawabata than any of those other translations on the shelf.

Dandelions was first published in the literary magazine *Shinchō* in twenty-two installments from June 1964 to October 1968, with two long gaps along the way—the first from July 1964 to February 1965, the second from March 1966 to November 1967. The final install-ment ran in *Shinchō* just two weeks before the Swedish Academy an-nounced that Kawabata would be the first Japanese author—in fact, the first author writing in a non-Western language—to be awarded the Nobel Prize in Literature. The translation presented in this book is based, however, not on those installments, but on an edited text of the entire unfinished novel that was printed in a special issue of *Shinchō* released in June 1972 to commemorate Kawabata's death, then published in book form, and then included in Kawabata's col-lected works. The revisions were made by Kawabata's son-in-law in accordance with notes Kawabata wrote on pages ripped from the magazine. Needless to say, we have no way of knowing what Kawabata himself might have done with these notes had the Nobel Prize and death not dragged him away from his writing, and had he had an opportunity to expand and revise the manuscript himself. Thus *Dandelions* remains unfinished not merely in the sense that it does not have an end, but also because entire sections of the existing text were bound to be moved, removed, or rewritten.

For the most part, the edited text of *Dandelions* is clean. One sentence allows us, however, a subtle glimpse of the messiness and indeterminacy of the process that created it. Halfway down page 79 in this English translation, we encounter this line: "She was thinking of her lover, Kuno, and how he liked to toy with her hair." This appears in the midst of the conversation Ineko and her mother have after the ping-pong match during which the teenage Ineko suddenly stops seeing the ball. It seems odd for Ineko to be thinking of Mr. Kuno here, since this scene takes place when Ineko is in eleventh grade, and although we are never told precisely when Ineko and Kuno became lovers, they don't appear to have been acquainted at this point—on page 92, Kuno reveals his ignorance of Ineko's ping-ponging, and both he and Ineko's mother seem to view Ineko's high school days as part of a past he and she do not share.

In fact, in the original *Shinchō* serialization, a full page of additional text separated "She was thinking of her lover, Kuno ..." from what, in this translation, is the following sentence: " 'That's the sort of girl you were,' her mother said. Thinking not of Kuno, of course, but of Ineko gathering blossoms." Kawabata's son-in-law deleted the passage because Kawabata had marked it with a note saying it "Happens later" (*ato no koto*). Presumably Kawabata lost track of the complex temporal layering in this part of the novel, and wrote a scene that could not have taken place when it does. The timing of this slip-up, in terms of the novel's serialization, lends credence to this supposition: a twenty-one month gap separated the thirteenth installment, which ended with Ineko's mother recalling how reluctant Ineko was to bathe with her after she slept with Kuno for the first time (page 69 of this translation), from the fourteenth, which began with Ineko's return from the ping-pong tournament (the first line on page 70). According to Kawabata's son-in-law, this long hiatus in the serialization of *Dandelions* was largely a result of Kawabata's hospitalization from January to March, 1966, for a severe case of hepatitis.

Dandelions is an intense, peculiar book—more so, perhaps, than Kawabata would finally have wanted it to be. It makes me think of a blurry photograph whose streaked colors and lack of clarity call to mind the hands gripping the camera, even though they are not there in the frame. If the cameraman had been able to retake the photo, we would have been left with a sharper, more focused image, but it would not have communicated the same messy, vibrant warmth. The publication of this translation offers us a chance, I hope, to see Kawabata as he has not been seen before in English—less polished, less settled.

I'll close with two notes regarding the translation itself. First, a minor but important point: after much discussion with the editor of this book (Barbara Epler, for whose sensitivity and thoughtfulness I am deeply grateful), I decided to have Mrs. Kitao know "how to speak English quite well" on page 22, rather than know "how to speak American quite well." The reference to "American" seemed liable to confuse readers unduly, or worse yet to register as a sign of puzzling ignorance on either Kawabata's part or mine. At the same, this one word seems to me to capture something of the atmosphere of the postwar moment Kawabata is describing, and to do so well enough to bear mentioning here. Second, a note about a name: "Mr. Kuno" could also be read "Mr. Hisano," and is, in fact, in the French translation of this book. I have decided to go with "Mr. Kuno" for two reasons: because it appears to be the more common reading, and because Kawabata counted among his acquaintances the writer

Kuno Toyohiko, whose name is written with the same characters. In a sense, it might have been better to take the same route as the French translator, privileging consistency. From another point of view, though, it seems appropriate in the case of this novel to let the uncertainty stand.

MICHAEL EMMERICH
LOS ANGELES, OCTOBER 2017